GW00374724

The Opposite of You

Sienna Waters

Published by Sienna Waters, 2020.

THE OPPOSITE OF YOU

First edition. April 2, 2020.

Copyright © 2020 Sienna Waters.

ISBN: 979-8223551614

Written by Sienna Waters.

Chapter One

Mac

I slid slowly into character. I smiled, held out my hand and commented on the weather. It was what was expected of me. The blonde smiled back and I felt the familiar shot of adrenaline as the woman looked me straight in the eye.

"Cassandra Wheeler," the blonde said, still pumping at my hand.

"Jennifer Leighton," I said, widening my smile just a little further. "Jen." I didn't stumble over the name. Never had. That had been one of my first lessons: choose a name that slips off your tongue. Jen was an identity I'd used more than once before.

"It's a beautiful building," Cassandra said. "Well kept, clean. Are the building fees a nightmare?"

I stepped back to allow the woman entry to the apartment. "Not at all," I said with a small grin. "All included in the rent."

"Wow. What a place."

I stood in the center of the large living room as the blonde spun around, taking in the tall windows, the high ceilings, the tastefully painted walls. It was quite the apartment. The pictures on the short term rental site really hadn't done it justice at all.

"It's a shame to leave it," I agreed. "But, well, I don't really have much choice. And I definitely can't afford to leave the place empty." I paused for a second, then took a step closer to the woman, creating a false intimacy. "You wouldn't like a coffee, would you? I'm dying for a cup."

Cassandra laughed. "You read my mind."

The blonde followed me to the breakfast bar overlooking the kitchen and I pulled two mugs out of a cupboard. I went for the right door, hand on the mugs immediately, I'd done my homework. I wasn't about to trip over something as simple as not being able to find the mugs in what was supposed to be my own apartment.

A fresh pot of coffee was bubbling on the counter, the smell permeating the apartment. The scent of cinnamon and fresh bread whirled around my nose, thanks to the bread rolls sprinkled with spice that I'd heated up in the oven earlier. Then ditched. I hate cinnamon. A minor expense, but an important one. People so often underestimate the power of smell when renting out a place. Not me though. No, Mac Seymour knows every trick in the book.

"So, if you don't mind me asking, why are you leaving this place?" the blonde said when her fingers were curled around a hot mug.

Time for the emotional sell. I needed to be careful here. Too much emotion and the mark gets jumpy, feels awkward and uncomfortable and eager to get away. Too little and they won't get drawn in, won't be hooked. It's a fine line.

"It's uh, well, I guess..." I pretended to stutter and turned away so that she couldn't see into my eyes. "My fiance and I brought this place together," I said.

"Ah."

There was a second when I thought maybe I'd misjudged the situation. But then her hand snaked out and patted me on the forearm, the sparkling ring on her finger glowing with newness. No misjudgment here then.

"It's fine, I'm okay, really," I said. "Just... well, being here is tough now and I need to move on and... well, you know how it is."

She tutted sympathetically. I held my tongue. Better a story too short then one too long, that's what my Uncle Frank always says. Sprinkle in too many details and you increase your chances of getting caught. Too many things that can be checked, too many lies to remember.

Besides, most people don't spill all the details at once, they savor some things for later, hold back the juicy parts in reserve for family and friends. It's only liars that feel the need to dot every i and cross every t, to fill in every gap.

"I'm so sorry," Cassandra said eventually.

I shrugged, wondering what she guessed had happened. In her head, there was a whole different story to my life. A story where my fiancé had died in a flaming wreck, or left me for his best friend, or jumped off the highway bridge just down the street. It didn't matter which of these she thought, of course, but I was curious nevertheless.

"Would you like to see the rest of the place?" I said, with exactly the right amount of forced cheerfulness to convey that I didn't want to discuss the thorny issue of my a fiancé anymore.

"Absolutely," she smiled with relief, excused from having to comfort a grieving stranger.

We wandered together through the airy apartment, me holding back a little, letting her explore by herself. Letting her fall in love with the neutral tones, the clean lines, the minimalistic feel that made the place look like it was out of some magazine. Occasionally, she tossed me a question, and I answered fluidly, fluently. This wasn't my first rodeo.

"I love this room," she said, stepping into the bedroom. "The windows, the view, the space. Wow, just wow."

I nodded, smiling mechanically. The room was huge. So huge that I figured you could fit my and Mia's entire studio in without a problem. I shivered a little.

Comparing the filth of the hovel I shared with my sister to this place was an unpleasant reminder of what I needed to go home to. I sighed. I'd treated myself to spending the night in the rental apartment last night. I'd had no choice but to rent overnight, so it would have been a waste not to. One night of clean sheets and nice views and big bath tubs. Really not long enough.

"I'm sorry," Cassandra said, patting my arm again. "This must be really painful for you."

It took me a second to realize that she meant renting out my little love nest, dealing with whatever had happened to my fake fiancé, piecing together a life shattered by... something. I gave her a small smile and backed out of the room, leaving her to the views.

She took her time. I glanced at my watch. Another prospective renter was coming in half an hour. Just enough time, as long as she made her decision soon. I felt the stirring of air as she came out of the bedroom. Time to get back to work.

"It's really a beautiful place," she said.

I detected the hint of doubt immediately. "We were very happy here," I said, laying it on a little thick. "The building fees are included, as are utilities."

"You must have a hundred people lining up to see this place."

I nodded and her face fell just a little, her confusion more than evident. Time to go in for the kill. "Listen, I have to be honest with you," I said. Never, ever trust someone that says they have to be honest with you. It nearly always means they're lying. "I've kind of already promised the place to someone."

A crease of frustration between her eyebrows. "You have?"

"Yes, but... Well, it's an older man. And I'd really prefer the place to have some life in it, a younger woman, a happy couple maybe. It would, I don't know, make me feel easier about leaving the place, I guess. Stupid, isn't it?"

"No, no, it's not stupid at all," she said.

I flashed her a conspiratorial smile. "The other guy didn't leave a deposit. He said he'd let me know by the end of the day. So I guess if you were to leave a deposit now, well, the place would be yours fair and square, wouldn't it?"

The doubt was gone now. Now that she knew that she might lose the place, she suddenly wanted it all the more. "Is a check okay?"

"Cash is best, if you don't mind," I said. "There's an ATM just at the corner. I'm moving out of state, you see, so I've already closed down my account here."

But she was already fiddling in her wallet for her ATM card. "Just give me five minutes."

It was eight minutes, to be precise. Those cold minutes whilst you're waiting for the mark to pay up are the hardest. They could change their mind at any second and the situation is no longer under your control. But she paid up, the full five hundred in cash, and left with my promises of emailed contracts ringing in her ears.

I breathed out a sigh as I rummaged in the kitchen cabinet for my bag. Carefully I stacked Cassandra's deposit with the other two bundles of cash that I'd earned today. Or extorted. Whichever you prefer, I'm not hiding what I do. I do what I have to to pay the bills.

Fifteen hundred bucks. And the place had only cost me two hundred to rent for the night. Add in the cost of coffee, bread rolls, and cinnamon and I was way ahead.

The doorbell rang. Way ahead and there was still one more mark to go. One more chance at an extra five hundred bucks. I hid my bag again and went to the door.

"Jennifer Leighton," I said, holding out my hand. "Jen."

The young red head in front of me grinned. "I love this place already," she said, practically squeaking with excitement.

"Oh, just you wait until you see inside," I smiled, ushering her in.

An easy mark. Who doesn't love an easy mark?

Chapter Two

Eleanor

The restaurant always strangely pleases me when it's empty. When it's closed, I mean, not just when we've got no customers. There's something satisfying about it being all clean, the chairs and tables being straight and in line, the glasses all washed, the floors all shining. It appeals to the more logical side of me, I suppose.

All of which implies that I like the place. That I'm not desperately trying to back my way out of what was, I now have to admit, a monumentally bad decision. The worst decision I've made in my business life. Hell, the worst I've made in my life period.

"So, what's the problem?"

The look on Addie's face as she waltzed in, shopping bags hanging from the crook of her elbow and eyes obscured by sunglasses, told me exactly how uninterested she was in this little meeting. Which should be surprising since we're technically business partners. But I've known Addie too long now to be surprised at her lack of interest in anything that doesn't involve her buying something shiny and expensive.

"The same problem we've had for the last year and a half," I said, trying to be calm and level.

"Ugh, money again."

She collapsed into a chair which creaked with her weight. Not that she's fat, the chairs are a flimsy designer affair that I hated from the first moment I saw them. But Addie persuaded me they were exactly what we needed. She's good at that. Persuading.

"Money again," I said. "We're just not getting anywhere close to the profits that we projected. And I want to understand why."

Addie shrugged. "Restaurants are a tough venture, you know that. They're up and down, profit margins are thin. But we're getting better all the time, more bookings, more catering orders. I think you're jumping the gun here."

She inched forward a little so that I could see the depths of her dark eyes, the way her lashes curled, the tiny dot on her nose that had once housed a ring. A ring that she'd removed three years ago stating that she was too old now for such nonsense. Three years ago when I thought it possible that Addie actually could mature.

"Jumping the gun?"

"Most restaurants close in their first year of doing business. You know that. We're long past that point. That's cause for celebration, surely?"

I sighed. The reason we were past that year-long deadline was simple. I'd pumped more money into the business. I'd increased my investment by half again. Addie was rummaging in one of her shopping bags.

"Look at this," she said, pulling out a black, sequinned shirt. "Tell me how amazing I'm going to look in this."

She held up the wisps of fabric and shot me that smile. The one that looked like a cat after getting into cream, the one that said she was satisfied, happy, indulged, the one that had once upon a time made my heart beat faster and my mouth dry up.

"Addie, we need to talk about this. It's important. If we don't start turning more of a profit soon, we—"

"We what?" Her eyes sparked sharp and she was glaring at me. "We close? I'm not falling for that, El. I'm not. This place is packed on the weekends. We're nowhere close to failing. So what if we're not making as much as we thought? The business is growing and you're being impatient."

That's another thing that Addie is good at. Making you feel like you're the one in the wrong even when you've done nothing. I bit my lip and took a breath before answering.

"There's no need to get dramatic about things. I just want to know more about the finances is all. I just... I want this place to succeed as much as you do. Really, I do."

Which was true. I wanted the place to succeed so that I could sell out and make my money back. There was no way after all of this that I was walking away with a loss. If I did, it would be the first loss I'd made in a business sense. And I figured I'd lost enough in the personal sense that I didn't need to double the pain.

"Okay," Addie said, stuffing the shirt back into her bag. "But I still think you're over-reacting."

I puffed out a breath of air. Over-reacting. Far from it. In fact, I was doing now what I should have done months ago. Would have done months ago. If I hadn't been blinded by Addie's smile, lulled by her touch.

"I've taken all the financial records," I said. "The books. I'm going to go through them, see what's what. Maybe we can make some cuts, increase our margins."

"The accountant?"

"Was happy to give things over to me," I said. Her eyes were narrowing as she considered the implications of this. "This could help," I said. "Really help."

Finally, she nodded. "Fine. If you want to do it, I guess. I mean, it's no skin off my nose, just more work for you." She gave me the side eye. "But then you always did like to spend your Saturday nights curled up with a good book, didn't you?"

The dig didn't hurt. Even when we were together I couldn't stomach Addie's party nights. The nights of drinking and clubbing and coming home at dawn with mascara smeared down your face. What she'd said was true, the difference between us being that she saw it as an insult and I didn't.

"I'll get to work on it," was all I said.

Addie gave an irritated sigh. One that I was obviously meant to comment on. I considered letting it go, but frankly, if there was something worse than an irritated Addie it was an Addie that wasn't the center of attention.

"What?"

"Oh, nothing."

A jolt of anger in my stomach. "What is it, Addie?" I asked again.

"Just..." Her eyes flickered to me then back to the tabletop. "Just I guess I thought this meeting was going to be about something else." She paused but I didn't speak. "About us," she added, finally.

"There's nothing to talk about there. There is no us."

Even now it hurt, it stung. But I didn't know if it hurt because we broke up or hurt because I'd misjudged her, made a bad decision. The fact that I'd chosen her, been so sure about her, and been wrong, left me shaken like the carpet was being pulled out from under my feet. Like I couldn't trust my own judgment anymore. Couple that with the restaurant investment spiraling downwards and I was beginning to think I'd lost my touch.

Me. Eleanor Shepherd. Losing her touch. Who'd have thought it? Straight As through high school, college and business school. I ticked every box, fulfilled every criteria, did exactly what I was supposed to do. All of which was meant to add up to success. All of which did add up to success. Until this. Until Addie and the restaurant and... I swallowed down the thoughts.

"No us?"

Addie's voice had gone up half an octave. A sign that she was about to yell or about to cry. I wasn't sure which.

"Anybody home?"

The shout came from the kitchen and I heard the back door clanking closed as footsteps came towards us. Addie rolled her eyes, denied her chance of a scene. Though depending on who was coming in, she might take a stab at getting her moment in the spotlight anyway.

"In here," I shouted back.

"Ah, there you are." Tom's hair was ruffled and his cheeks pink from the outside air. He was grinning and looked all of fifteen as he came into the dining room. "I'll just get the coffee machine switched on and open up the shutters," he said. "Then I can get you both a cup if you want one?"

I really should have turned the machine on myself. I knew that it needed time to warm up before opening. "That'd be nice."

"Yeah," Addie said, pushing back her chair and scooping up her shopping bags.

There would be no scene today. If it had been Kyla, our pretty blonde Australian waitress then Addie might have gone for it. But not Tom. She had no reason to want to impress Tom. Men had never been her weak point.

She disappeared off into the back and Tom rattled the shutters open and let the afternoon light flood into the dining room. Addie's chair was crooked now, the restaurant was no longer perfect and quiet. And my hatred for the place burned a little brighter.

"Make mine a latte," Addie shouted through to Tom.

Not for the first time I wondered why I'd done this. Why I'd fallen for Addie. Why I'd invested in the restaurant.

"Want a latte too?" asked Tom.

I shrugged. I couldn't trust myself to make the big decisions in life, so how the hell was I supposed to make the little ones? I felt my palms getting sweaty.

"I'll make it a double macchiato," Tom said, grinning at me. "You like those."

I nodded, glad that the decision had been taken out of my hands.

Chapter Three

Mac

It was still light out, the cold making my cheeks burn when I made my way home. Home. A loaded word if there ever was one. I clomped up the rickety stairs and made my way along the terrace that stretched across the front of the second floor of the building.

Terrace. Another word that conjures up pictures it shouldn't. This terrace is a concrete shelf littered with needles and trash, looking out over a piece of scrubland equally littered. Not exactly the grandest of places. Still, we had a roof over our heads. And I had fifteen hundred bucks in my bag. Not a bad day's work.

The front door had a hole at the bottom. Someone had been kicking it. I rattled my key in the lock, jamming against the door with my shoulder until it opened. And I knew as soon as the door opened.

Addiction has a smell. It's a dirty smell, but one that's sweet and clingy as well. A smell that I grew up with, an unmistakable one.

"You're back soon."

She'd tried, I'll give her that. She had clothes on, was propped up on the uneven couch, the TV blaring in a corner. But even with the blinds closed her pupils were like pinpricks.

"You're high."

"And you're early."

I took deep breaths. Choosing battles, that what it was about. Mia shouldn't be high and I wanted to know where she got the money from. But then again, I didn't want to hear what she'd had to do to score, because after everything she was still my big sister and I didn't want the pictures in my head that would accompany her explanations.

"Had a good day," I said, trying to make myself sound happy, light even. "Fancy a pizza for dinner?"

Her eyes were boring into me and her hair was lank and stringy and hanging down. "What kind of good day?"

All about the money. It always was when she was like this. Always about thinking where she was going to get the next fix from. I could handle it, really I could. She wasn't always this bad. She could go days, weeks even. Sometimes she got methadone from the clinic on the next block. But somehow, she always fell back into that sweet-smelling hole of addiction. And I was terrified that one day she wouldn't climb back out.

"Fifteen hundred," I said, clasping my bag tight to my side.

"Make ten times that if you worked with Frank," she grunted.

"Maybe."

I didn't say more, didn't have to. If she was in her right mind she wouldn't have said that, wouldn't have wanted me to join our uncle in whatever shit he was into right now. Dealing, trafficking, big time crime.

"Make more if you didn't dress like you were a desperate teenager on the pull."

The mean part always came after a while. She must have taken around lunch time, a little after. While I was showing beautiful, blonde Cassandra around an apartment that I had no right to rent out. While I was making money.

"What's that supposed to mean?"

"It's supposed to mean that bleach blonde hair with pink tips, tank tops and tattoos don't exactly make you look like you're over thirty."

Which was kind of the point. I knew I looked younger than I was. I liked the half-pink hair. But then, dressing a little better, looking a little more... suburban, trustworthy, could make it easier to grift.

No. No. I wasn't going to be in the game long enough this time for it to matter. I really wasn't. We were almost there, almost ready, we almost had enough. The beginnings of enough, anyway.

"You're a pleasure to be around this afternoon," was all I said.

Mia snorted and her pin-prick gaze went back to the TV. An un-seeing gaze. Whatever was playing in her head, coursing through her veins, was more interesting than the infomercial on the screen.

"You didn't answer me about the pizza," I said.

I was walking towards the alcove with the bed. The bed we took it in turns to sleep in, a curtain blocking it off from the rest of the grubby studio, the only really vaguely private place we had.

"Whatever," Mia said.

She's my sister. I love her. She gave me everything, she was my everything. After mom left Mia was all I had. She raised me and okay, yeah, she probably could have done better. But she could have done a whole lot worse. She could have left too. Which is why I didn't fight her, I didn't answer back, I just gritted my teeth and dropped my bag on the bed.

I waited a few minutes, wanting to be sure that she wasn't paying attention, wanting her to slip into that semi-comatose state that the drugs will tempt her into, before I started scrabbling around for the box.

The box.

The box was the most precious thing I owned by far. It might not look like much, it wasn't much, just a battered shoe box that once held a pair of men's brogues. But it held our future. Mine and Mia's. Because with what was in the box we could start paying off the debt. With what was in the box we could make the down-payment on Mia's rehab.

For a second I imagined the place from the brochure. Calm and white with gardens and a pool, and more importantly with the best success rate in the tri-state area for getting junkies off their junk.

And I knew that the rehab payment would come first. Before the debts, the money mom owed and we inherited, the money Mia spent trying to keep us together and fed and housed, the money we owed to a dozen different creditors.

Because once Mia was better, once she was Mia again, then there'd be two of us to make the decisions, two of us to earn, and we'd pay off the debts that much quicker.

And because then I'd have someone to share things with. Someone to take some of the responsibility off my shoulders.

I pulled the cash out of my bag. Fifteen hundred bucks. Three deposits. Not four. Because the eager red-head hadn't been as easy a mark as I'd thought. She'd refused to leave a deposit until her boyfriend could see the place. She'd refused to make a decision alone, wanting to share the responsibility with someone else. And I was angry, mad, but inside I understood.

Having someone else there must be nice.

I'd buried the box at the far back of a drawer, one loaded with denim skirts and fishnets, a drawer I knew Mia would show no interest in. She was more the yoga pants and sweatshirt kind of girl.

My fingers plowed under the fabric, searching for that hard edge. And when I didn't find it my pulse quickened.

"Calm, calm. Look again," I whispered.

But still nothing. I started pulling clothes out of the drawer, started flinging them on the bed, getting more desperate, more sweaty, more panicky as the drawer emptied.

Shit. Fuck.

I pulled the drawer to its limit, sliding my hand down the back, bending down to reach all the way down into empty space. And then I saw the corner of the box just peeking from under the bed.

I knew before I opened it, before I touched it even, that it would be empty.

It wasn't the first time.

I should have taken it with me. I knew that. I should have looked after it more carefully. Because this was the problem with having someone else. Sure, sharing the responsibility for things must be nice. But then you have to trust them too, don't you?

Anger was sour in my mouth and my stomach ached. Mia was still in front of the TV, oblivious, eyes half-closed. There was no point in talking to her about this. She'd deny it, she always did. Even though we both knew where the money had gone.

And there was no point in demanding it back. Because it was gone. Gone into little plastic baggies that would be hidden in places too sneaky for me to find. Baggies that I didn't want to find because I had no interest in what was inside.

Fuck it.

We'd gotten so close this time.

I stood up, trying to control my anger, stalking back out into the living room, yanking at the front door.

"Hey, what about that pizza?" Mia yelled.

I slammed the door to cut off her voice. I didn't want to hear it.

See, in the end, it's better to be alone. Better to work alone, to live alone, to trust alone. Because there's only one person in the world that you can trust and that's yourself.

I hesitated at the top of the stairs and thought about going back, thought about trying to reason with her. Maybe she could sell the drugs, return them somehow. But trusting an addict to do that was even stupider than trusting them not to find a wad of cash hidden in a shoebox.

No. I needed some time alone.

I skidded back down the stairs, anger chewing through my bones, blinking back tears that I refused to cry.

Chapter Four

Eleanor

The problem was that I always did the right thing. I knew that. Walking down the street, shopping bag swinging from my hand, I knew that I was in a prison of my own making.

The bag was light, though I'd already bought what I'd been sent to get. Parsley. An essential, I'd been told. Though how the hell the restaurant had managed to run out of something so essential I had no idea.

Better planning. Better planning and logistics and organization. That would be what made a difference. That would be what made the place as profitable as we'd planned.

Because I hadn't walked into this quite as blindly as it might seem. I'd insisted on business plans and profit forecasts and everything else that my career as an investment banker and then as an investor had taught me were necessary. And they'd all looked good. But now things weren't good.

My first failure was a bitter pill to swallow. One that I was still struggling to get down my throat. One that I really, truly didn't want to accept.

I crossed the street diagonally, knowing that I was going out of my way, but unable to resist the temptation to see it. Who knew when it was going to be gone? Maybe it could be gone now. My stomach clenched and I hurried a little, feet trip-tripping on the sidewalk, needing to know whether it was there or not.

I needn't have worried. Before I reached the window I could see that it was still there. Tall and white with slashes of pink and violet. Not the colors I'd have chosen myself. Still beautiful though.

My nose almost pressed up against the glass of the baker's window I was like a child before Christmas staring at the tiered wedding cake.

Time lost meaning as I stood and stared, my brain whirling with ideas. Surely the cake had been layered and supported with internal dowels before being frosted to perfection. But just how had those tiny roses been done? Over and over again I experimented with ways to get flowers so neat and small, and over and over again I failed.

I didn't spend all of my free time reading, whatever Addie might think. No, I spent a fair amount of time baking. It was what I loved, what I'd always loved. What I'd considered making my profession until it had been made clear to me that more was expected of me. More was expected of Eleanor Shepherd than fooling around in the kitchen covered in flour.

It was nothing like the cake I'd imagined for Addie and I. No, our wedding was to have been elegant and understated. A simple two-tier cake with bright white fondant and silver accents. That had been the plan.

The sharpness of it hit me again, almost taking my breath away. There would be no cake, no wedding. Because there was no Addie and I. Because I had failed again.

I clutched the shopping bag in my hand and dragged myself away from the window, marching down the street towards the restaurant.

It had been inevitable, I suppose. The failure, I mean. Or do I mean failures? Inevitable in that failure was a part of life, it happened to everyone. Except me. I had literally never failed at a thing in my life. I'd made the decisions that had been expected of me, and I'd reaped the rewards.

Don't get me wrong, the rewards were great. There was plenty of money in the bank, enough to fund the restaurant fifty times over if I felt like it. There was a savings account with more than enough to place the deposit on the house that Addie and I had been choosing. Somewhere nice. Somewhere safe. Somewhere suburban.

The pressures were great too though. The pressure to do well, to succeed again, each time to do better than the last. To live up to the expectations that everyone had of me.

That's kind of a lie. I thrived under expectations. I enjoyed the challenge of meeting them and thrilled with the adrenaline of exceeding them. Until now.

The restaurant came into view, the windows starting to steam from the warmth inside. It was too cold still for the outside tables to be filled. But they were set up anyway, the bastion of the last few hard-core smokers who insisted on having their coffee in the freezing air so they could tend to their drug habit.

I had always been so concerned with what people thought of me. Even now, a large part of the reason that I wasn't walking away, that I was still working with Addie, was because I didn't want people to think that I'd failed. I wanted to at least have some semblance of success.

I pushed open the door and the bell rang and Tom looked up from taking an order and I realized that I really should have gone in through the back door.

See? My judgment had suffered. I made bad decisions now. Even the little ones. Maybe it was shock, maybe it was like... like falling off a horse and not getting immediately back on.

I hurried through the restaurant trying to be unobtrusive but my eye was caught by a flash of pink at one of the side tables.

The girl was sitting alone. Unusual for this time in the evening. It was not quite dark yet, but we were still getting the early birds in, the couples who wanted to eat before going to the movies or the theater. You learn a lot about people's habits in the restaurant trade, and solo eaters tended to come in either very early or very late. As though they didn't want to be confronted by couples and groups, didn't want to be reminded of their solitude.

Her hair was pale blonde, almost white, with bright pink tips. She'd pulled a leather jacket on over a tank top, a jacket that she hadn't taken off despite the warmth inside. Tight jeans encased her legs and as she reached for a napkin I saw the flash of a tattoo on the inside of her wrist.

That. Her. What would that be like? To be so free of concern about others, so free in yourself, that you dye your hair white and pink? That you eat alone in a restaurant? That you order two drinks simultaneously. I could clearly see two different glasses in front of her. A Mai-Tai and a Martini if I had to guess.

Spikes of jealousy ran through my torso. And it was ridiculous. Here I was, wealthy, accomplished, well-educated, with everything I had ever wanted, more or less. And I was jealous of a girl with pink hair. Jealous because I suspected she might have made better decisions in her life than I had. Because she was free of what others thought, because she pleased herself and only herself.

I willed her to look up. But she didn't. So I stared and consequences be damned.

"Got the parsley?" Tom was whisking by me, order pad in hand, talking over his shoulder as he went.

I held up the bag in my hand, letting it dangle limply from one finger.

"Best get it into the kitchen, they're holding up plates right now," he said, walking backward through the kitchen door himself.

I took one more look at the girl. An air of confidence surrounded her. Was she happier than I was? The holes in her jeans and the state of her jacket told me that she was hardly rich. The crueler side of me was already wondering how she was going to pay her bill. We're a small restaurant and profit margins might be thin, but we're not exactly cheap. Yet I still thought she probably was happier than I. And that hurt.

I pushed through the door to the kitchen, tossing my bag to Tom who caught it deftly and passed it along the line.

No sign of Addie. She'd be primping herself now. Smoothing lipstick on in front of the bathroom mirror, making herself look shiny and glowing and almost, if you squinted, like one of those second-rate celebrities you see on TV in reality shows. That was the part that entranced her about all this. Being able to gossip behind the bar, being able to kiss regular customers on both cheeks and exclaim that she didn't see them nearly enough. That and the new outfits she got to buy.

I sighed. I should leave. Go home. Start going through the books. But the thought of the pink-haired girl had me a little on edge.

Perhaps tonight I could make a small step. Just a little one.

A drink at the bar, maybe.

Sitting alone, legs crossed, cold glass in hand. Looking like I didn't care.

My heart hammered at the thought. Drinking alone. Who did that?

I did. I decided. As of when, asked the voice at the back of my head. As of now, I told myself firmly.

Chapter Five

Mac

"Want a side with that?"

"Fries would be good."

The young, blonde waiter smiled at me and I smiled back. Not a full-on kind of grin, just enough to be polite.

Don't draw attention to yourself. That's a big rule. Don't be rude, sure, but don't be too polite either. I mean, I guess some people would say that I'm drawing attention to myself by having wild hair colors, but that's not really the same thing.

People see what they want to see. When they look at me they see someone unthreatening. Sure, I've got pink hair and a leather jacket, but I'm a girl and a small one at that. I'm immediately dismissed because I pose no physical danger. It doesn't matter what color my hair is.

"And maybe another drink?"

I shook my head. It doesn't do to have too much alcohol. And to be honest, ordering two drinks at the same time was drawing more attention to myself than I should have. But I wasn't intending to come back here.

"Then I'll put that through to the kitchen," he said, still smiling.

He was cute. Not really my type. But cute. I've been with guys, but in general, I prefer women. I prefer the gentleness, the softness. Sometimes though, you gotta do what you gotta do to get ahead. So in my line of business, you don't get to be too picky.

I sipped at my Mai-Tai. It was good, tart on my tongue. The restaurant was fancy, fancier than I'd normally have chosen. But I'd walked until my feet ached and it had been the first decent place I saw.

And I needed decent. Up market.

Here's something that a lot of people don't get. Ripping people off isn't fun. It's not something I do because I like it. I do it because I have to. And because of that, there have to be rules. Rules about what's okay and what's not.

Call it differentiating between shades of grey.

For example, on the corner of this very street there's a little deli. Checkered red and white tablecloths, the awning striped and fraying at the edges. Even the look of it tells you that you're going to have one of the greatest Reubens of your life when you step through the door.

But I didn't. Step through the door, I mean. Because you don't take from people like that. You don't take from those that are struggling just as hard as you are. Like I said, there are rules.

A fancy place like this though, that's okay. Not okay-okay, but okay.

Like I said, different shades of grey.

I sat and waited, calmly and quietly. I didn't need entertainment. No book, no phone. Just me and my eyes and ears, that was enough. You miss a lot by being distracted.

"Meal will be right up," the waiter said, sliding by my table.

Maybe he was flirting, maybe he was angling for a better tip.

I didn't regret storming out of the house. If I'd stayed I would have had regrets, regrets for blaming Mia for something she couldn't control. That was a tough lesson, learning that Mia wasn't choosing to do this. At least not anymore. Now it was controlling her.

I was angry, I was disappointed, I had a rolling ball of negativity and blackness and spite in my stomach. But I'd walked off the immediate effects.

Yes, I could have yelled and shouted and punched. But where would that have got me? The only thing to do was start again. So here I was. I was going to have a decent meal for once. And then I was going to go home, make sure that Mia was safe, go to bed, and get started on a hustle in the morning.

The only thing I could do.

"Here we go."

He slid the plate in front of me and my stomach growled. Meat juices were already oozing out of the steak and I could nearly feel it in my mouth.

"Thank you." Polite, but not too polite.

Life is always better with a full stomach. The restaurant was starting to get busy and I kept a running tally of those coming in and out. It becomes habit after a while, knowing who is in a place and who isn't. That and plotting an escape route every time you walk in somewhere.

In fact, life got so good, I broke down and ordered myself some dessert. Screw it. It had been a shitty afternoon and I deserved it.

I was looking around for the cute blonde waiter when I saw her.

Sitting at the bar, legs crossed, hair up, drink in hand. My eye got stuck on her. There was something about her that drew my gaze. Okay, she was attractive, but it wasn't just that. She was... put together. Organized. In a way that was hard to define.

Long dark hair swept up to show her neck, skin pale and soft-looking, profile sharp and even. She was the kind of woman that you had to look twice at.

Looking was all though. Her pants probably cost more than my entire wardrobe.

But a throb went through my stomach anyway. Lust, desire, whatever. There was something about that hairstyle that really made me want to mess it up.

Dessert appeared, this time the waiter smiled but said nothing. Out of small talk, I guess.

And under my lashes, I was still watching the woman. Watching until someone else came, someone sweeping in, stepping behind the bar. Blonde, blowsy, big makeup, but pretty in her own way. And whoever the second woman was, it was obvious that she and my femme fatale at the bar were somehow involved.

The easiest way to tell if two people are intimate to wait until one gives something to the other. If the other doesn't say thank you, they're involved. Simple. The only people you don't thank are those closest to you. Weird, but true.

And as I spooned brownie and ice cream into my mouth my suspicions were proven. The blonde handed a set of keys to the dark-haired one, and not a word was said.

I've never had that. That kind of intimacy I mean. Don't get me wrong, there have been girlfriends. But more of the 'stop by after a night at the bar and get your rocks off' kind of girlfriend, if you get my meaning.

Not like I had time for anything else. Besides, living with my sister wasn't exactly conducive to a long term relationship.

And there was a spiky feeling inside me that I couldn't quite identify as I scooped up dessert. Kind of like brain freeze, but in my stomach.

It took me the rest of the brownie to figure out the feeling was jealousy. I was jealous of the woman with the expensive pants and the blowsy girlfriend. Who'd have thought it?

I let my spoon clatter into the glass. I was done here. But I couldn't make a move too soon. I had to be careful.

The most dangerous part of a dine and dash is rather obviously the dashing part. Move too soon and the waiter is already on his way to collect your plate or offer the bill or coffee or whatever. Leave too late and the waiter's hovering around waiting for you to leave.

Fortunately, I had this down to a fine art.

"Everything good here?" the waiter asked, picking up my desert glass and smearing ice cream on his thumb.

"Perfect," I said. I picked up my glass and took a sip so that he could see it was still half-full. Reason enough for me to be at the table for another few minutes at least. "Could you tell me where the bathroom is?"

"Right back there," he said, pointing to a black door in the back wall.

Bingo. Now I had a reason to be standing up even though I hadn't yet paid.

"Can I get you something else? Another drink maybe? A coffee?"

Jesus, he was handing me this on a plate. If only people knew how easy they made it to rip them off. I held up the half full drink again. "Maybe in a while," I said, intimating that I might be staying even longer.

He grinned and carried my dessert dish away. Definitely working on a big tip. Not the flirtatious type, I decided. I stretched my legs under the table and took a long swill of one of my drinks. Then I darted a glance at the bathroom door, signaling my intentions whilst simultaneously checking the location of the waiter and anyone else that might be about to stop me.

I stood up with purpose. I'd left my jacket on, a good move, because picking up your coat when you're ostensibly on the way to the toilet sends entirely the wrong message. A deep breath, that familiar flood of adrenaline, and then I was off. Not running, but not strolling either. My steps sounded loud on the tiled floor as I veered away from the bathroom and approached the front door.

Chapter Six

Eleanor

Sitting at a bar with a drink in your hand isn't particularly interesting. In fact, I was thoroughly failing to see why people did it at all. And my little rebellion, my little gasp of freedom, wasn't aided by the fact that pretty much as soon as I sat down, Addie chose to make an appearance.

"You're staying?" She looked far from pleased.

"For now."

"Might as well take these then." She passed me a set of keys. "New set for the back door and one for the safe."

I slid them into my pocket and drank a little more of my drink.

"It doesn't have to be like this," Addie said, leaning forward.

"What doesn't?"

"This. Us. We don't have to be like this."

"I believe we've already discussed today that there is no us."

"For Christ's sake, El, I've apologized. How many more times do I need to say I'm sorry? I made a mistake, okay? Have you never made one?"

I wasn't about to tell her that she was the biggest mistake I'd made. That everything surrounding her was a mistake. So I said nothing. She huffed at this. But I felt safe enough in the knowledge that she wouldn't push her luck in the restaurant, not now that people were starting to come in. People she knew.

She was about to turn away from me, her attention was gone, I could feel it leaking away from me. But then she frowned.

"What?"

She held up a hand for a second, quietening me as her frown deepened. Somewhere I could hear footsteps, and I knew that they were heading for the door.

"We've got a runner," Addie said.

It happens. It happens to every restaurant. Some people think we're just here to provide them with free food. Some do it for the adrenaline rush, I suppose. Some might have legitimately forgotten their wallets or had their cards denied, though why they think running out without paying the bill is a solution to this, I don't know.

We take it into account, a certain amount of loss. So there was absolutely no reason at all to do what I did. Not in the slightest. But I was doing it before I realized it was happening.

My brain made the instant connection. I knew that it was the girl with pink and blonde hair. I'd even wondered how she could afford to be here.

And my legs were already hopping off the bar stool, I was already gaining my balance. And then I was moving.

Mac

Don't run until you hit the sidewalk. But once your feet collide with the concrete, then you bust your gut to get as far away as possible.

I knew that. I've been doing this since I was a kid. And it wasn't like I wasn't fit enough to escape.

My feet were pounding down the sidewalk, my breath was coming in deep, even gasps. I was working my arms, pumping away with everything that I was worth.

Which is when I heard shouting. Not unusual. What was unusual was the footsteps, the sound of the chase.

Now let's get this straight. Rich restaurants don't chase down dashers. They just don't. It's part of the reason we choose them. Expensive restaurants have a loss policy, they accept that a certain amount of their profit is going to be wasted, by inefficient cooks, by over-generous bartenders, and sometimes by people like me.

But it's not worth chasing us down.

I put on a burst of speed but the feeling in my gut was that I'd screwed this up. Really screwed up this time.

Eleanor

Four years of cross country in high school and four years on the college track team. I wasn't exactly a team player, so lacrosse and soccer were out. Running though, that was something I could excel at, and something that involved me only relying on myself. The perfect choice.

And even in heels, even in dress pants with my hair up and my makeup done, it came back to me so naturally. My stride evened out, my feet hit the ground, I guarded my breathing and sped up.

At the back of my head though, there was still that little voice, the sensible one, the one asking what the hell I thought I was doing.

I didn't need to chase this girl. I didn't need to be doing this. People were looking at me. And not necessarily in a good way. They were looking at me in a 'she might just be insane' kind of way. The kind of way that made my skin crawl and my stomach flip over. I was, as my mother would have said, 'making a spectacle of myself,' by far the worst sin a lady could commit. Worse even than failing a class or getting pregnant.

Her hair was like a beacon and I could see that I was gaining. I lengthened my stride. I was going to catch her.

Why? I had no idea. I was just doing this. The fitting end to a shitty day. There was no reasoning, no thought behind it. The only thing that was driving me was the thought of grabbing hold of that damn jacket and taking the kid to task.

Don't steal. Don't lie. Don't cheat.

It's not difficult to live a good life. All you have to do is be good, be nice, be honest.

Mac

Wanna know how I screwed the pooch?

It's simple. Know your enemy.

Knowledge is power, end of story. Knowing who is in a room, knowing how to escape from that room, knowing what someone's maiden name is, or what their keycode is.

But I'd made my decision in a hurry, I hadn't been thinking straight. I'd been angry and disappointed and I'd messed up.

Ordinarily, I'd know the area so well that I'd have a half-dozen bolt-holes, a handful of places that I could run through or into or behind to avoid this very circumstance. But not here. Not in this part of town. This part of town was pricey, too rich for my blood.

But they weren't supposed to chase me.

I'd been complacent. Uncle Frank would have my head for this.

He's family, sure. And he can generally be relied upon to send someone to bail me out when the occasion arises. But for this, there was no way. He'd be so ashamed I didn't think he'd look me in the eye for a year.

My breath was coming harsh and raw in my throat. I willed myself forward, faster, faster. But my legs weren't responding. The messages weren't getting through. I literally couldn't find another ounce of speed.

I was growling with frustration, my heart pounding out of my chest. A dumpster was coming up, an alley beside it, that could be my saving grace. An alley, a fence, a short climb. Surely whoever this was wasn't going to follow me into the dirt and grime and darkness of an alley.

Maybe it was the blonde waiter. Maybe it was him.

I gathered every particle of energy left inside me and forced myself to move.

And then I felt something pulling at me.

A hand on my jacket.

Eleanor

It felt like every eye in the street was on me. I could feel the attention and it was cutting into me, painful and unwanted.

But she was just there. I was about to get her. I wasn't even breathing that hard. She dodged around a man and pushed herself to go faster, but I knew she wouldn't, couldn't.

I didn't stretch my arm out just yet, though I was pretty sure I could grab her. I let the chase go on for a second longer than it really needed to, enjoying the feel of the sidewalk under my feet, not knowing what I was going to do when I caught her.

And then I was almost parallel with her and had no choice but to reach out and pull at her jacket.

She stopped, breath tearing at her lungs, bending over, trying desperately to breathe. It gave me time to take hold of her upper arm, to hold her more tightly.

And then she looked up. Her eyes met mine.

My first thought wasn't a thought at all. It was a solid rush of heat that made my skin prickle with its intensity.

My second thought was that this was no girl at all. Up close, eye to eye, she was a woman. Definitely a woman.

My third thought, as those hazel and green-flecked eyes glared into mine was that I wanted her.

"Let me go." She squirmed and struggled.

But I held on. Harder than I needed to.

Chapter Seven

Mac

You can't control for everything. Sometimes the mark gets a phone call that takes his attention away from you right when you need it. Sometimes there's the ghost flash of a cop car at the end of an alleyway that spooks you. Sometimes it rains when you need sun or the other way around. Expecting the unexpected is bullshit. How are you supposed to expect it if it's unexpected? Isn't the very definition of unexpected that it's not expected?

She was holding tight onto me and my breath was coming in gasps and a hot flush was flooding through my body. I'd have sworn for a second that she was going to kiss me, that the sticky, breathless intimacy between us was more than just a vigilante catching a thief.

And another part of me, a part that I usually buried deep, was telling me that this was incredible. Incredible because the neat, put-together woman in heels sitting at the bar was now holding me by the arm after having chased me four blocks down the street. Incredible because if I'd have had to choose a Superman out of that restaurant she'd have been my second to last choice, just ahead of that blonde bartender girlfriend of hers. Incredible because even if she hadn't been holding me I didn't think that I could run.

"Come with me."

She was pulling at me, turning me, leading me back the way I'd come and as soon as her eyes were gone, as soon as she was looking elsewhere, the spell was broken. I let myself be led, relaxing the muscles in my arm in the hopes that if I did she would relax her grip. Attention on the street was gone, people going back to their normal lives. Now was my chance.

But I didn't take it. That grip was too strong, or so I told myself.

"I'M CALLING THE POLICE."

"No, ma'am, please. It was an honest mistake."

Polite. Don't fight, don't curse, don't struggle. When all else fails, try and talk your way out. The kitchen was clattering behind me, the hissing of hot pans and the clink of plates. The smells made my mouth water even though I'd just eaten.

"There's nothing honest about you."

I couldn't exactly fault her judgment on that. At least not at this point.

She was leaning back, arms crossed, china blue eyes studying me. My eyes darted to the door to my right. A kitchen hand was draped across the opening smoking a cigarette. There was a set of swing doors ahead and to my left. But the constant flow of traffic in and out meant that that wasn't a clear exit. Besides, I'd still have to navigate the restaurant itself if I went that way.

"I forgot my wallet," I said. "Honestly, I did. I know I made the wrong decision. I shouldn't have run. But I got embarrassed. I'm truly sorry."

She didn't buy it. I could see she didn't. I could also see that allowing myself to be dragged into the kitchen was not my greatest move. There'd be no clear escape from here. Jesus, what was wrong with me?

This was all Mia's fault. She'd put me off my game, made me impulsive, made me angry. And now look at me.

The woman was scowling at me now. Her skin was porcelain perfect, her hair tidy despite her run. She was exactly the kind of girl I hated. The kind of girl that never did wrong. The kind of girl that never struggled for anything. The kind of girl that was perfection personified. I kind of wanted to spit in her face.

"What woman walks more than a block from her front door before realizing she's forgotten her bag?" she said.

Not her, obviously. Because little Miss Perfect would never make a mistake like that. A block without a bag, lord, what a scandal. Wait. Without a bag.

Shit.

My bag was lying on the bed. The money was lying in the bag. Mia was sitting on the couch. I blinked, forcing my tears back down, not letting the emotion out. How could I have been so stupid? I'd made a mistake by leaving the box in the house, sure, but I'd just done the exact same thing again, leaving my bag where Mia could get at it.

"There's no point crying about this."

"I'm not crying," I said through gritted teeth.

She moved a little. I gulped back the lump in my throat but my skin was prickling. This was getting to her. Okay, okay, I had her number now.

"It's just..." I let a little of that emotion cloud my voice, a hint of a sob. "It's just been so hard being alone, and, and... I was so hungry. And I know it's unforgivable, I do know." I sniffed and blinked but didn't allow the tears to come out. If I did, God knew how I'd stop them again.

"I'm calling the police."

Crap. Not the intended effect. Had I misread her? She had her phone in her hand already.

"Please."

Just that one word. It slipped out before I could stop it, sounded more real than anything I'd said in days, weeks. A whole weight of a shitty life was hanging in that word and it bobbed between us.

"What's your name?"

It came out of nowhere and I was committed before I could stop myself. The question was so unexpected that I answered with the truth. "Mac."

She nodded. "Eleanor, Eleanor Shepherd."

Why the introductions? I took a half step back until I was perched against a counter. I looked left and right again, just to be sure that I couldn't make a break for it.

"I'm the owner."

"Half-owner." This new voice was softer, lighter and the blonde from behind the bar appeared. "Half-owner," she said again. "And who's this?"

Eleanor, Eleanor. Such an... old name. Not one I'd choose myself, and I had a lot of practice choosing names. But it fit her. Fit the slight old fashioned sense about her. Eleanor's cheeks had tightened when the blonde had come in. Tightened further when the word 'half-owner' was spoken. An argument between the two of them? Trouble in paradise. Maybe. I filed away the thought, it could be useful to me.

"The dine and dash," Eleanor said.

The blonde's eyes sparkled with curiosity. "You caught her?"

"And now I'm deciding what to do with her."

I stayed silent, watching the two of them. Two against one was not good odds. Unless I could turn them against each other, get one on my side. I thought about Eleanor's hand on my arm and a shiver of warmth went through me. But the blonde was staring at me with interest.

"What's your story?" she said.

"Addie, let it go. I'm just going to call the cops," said Eleanor. "It's the right thing to do."

Now I had to speak. "I'm really sorry, truly I am. Couldn't I like, wash dishes or something?" Okay, I was getting desperate. But I really didn't need trouble with the police. Not over something as simple as this. Eleanor's jaw was relaxing a little. She was being presented with another option, a way of saving face. I was getting to her. "I'll work all night, up until closing."

"It's the traditional method of punishing dine and dash-ers," the blonde, Addie, put in.

I gave her a half smile. Someone on my side. Finally. The two of them made the cutest couple, Eleanor so dark, Addie so blonde. Addie laid a hand on Eleanor's arm as if to encourage her. She'd come over to my side fast, but I couldn't see anything in this for her. There was more at play here than I understood.

"Please, give me a chance." I had every intention of ducking out the door the second her back was turned. But she didn't have to know that.

"Fine." She sounded somehow unsure of herself. "The sink's over there. If you have problems, ask someone for help. I'll be back to check on you later." She turned to the blonde. "What do you need?"

"Jo's here," Addie said. "Just thought you'd like to know. And petty cash has dried up. Got any spare change?"

"For what?"

"Lemons. Jesus, why does it matter?"

And there was definitely something going on here. Something between the two of them. I'd assumed they were a couple. Now it seemed they were a couple in trouble.

"How much?"

"Couple of hundred should do it."

Aha. Addie wanted cash. I scented troubled immediately. Two hundred bucks for lemons, as if.

"For lemons?" Eleanor said.

Addie rolled her eyes. "And for the deliveries in the morning."

"Addie, you have to keep better track..." Eleanor trailed off as she saw me still standing there. "Get to washing dishes before I change my mind."

"Yes, ma'am."

I moved slowly over to the sink keeping a close eye on the back door as I did so. The kitchen hand was about done with his smoke. My time was coming. I could almost feel the fresh air on my skin. Eleanor and Addie were arguing behind me. They were distracted. The perfect opportunity was coming and I could sense it, feel it, my heart starting to beat a little harder.

The kitchen hand turned to come back inside and I was judging the distance between me and the door and already taking a breath, calming myself before the run.

Eleanor covered the two strides in a millisecond, banging the security gate shut and slipping a key into the lock. The doorway was now covered by steel bars, a gap of no more than two inches between them. Enough to let in the cooler air, not enough to let me out.

The keys jingled in her pocket as she walked away, still talking to Addie.

Chapter Eight

Eleanor

I was still taken off-guard by that momentary flash of wanting. Holding that woman, pulling her close enough to me to kiss. It had been a natural reaction, I told myself. Biology. That was all. It wasn't like I was actually attracted to the thief. As if.

"Here."

I handed crisp bills to Addie who took them and immediately slid them into her pocket. I almost followed up with a warning about spending the cash, accounting for it. But I bit my tongue. Addie was a big girl, she knew how the business worked.

"Thanks." Addie turned to leave. "Jo's at the bar."

Jo. El. Addie liked nicknames, as though saying a full name was too much work for her. It didn't matter to her that I preferred being called Eleanor. Nor that Joanna preferred Joanna. It was such a little thing, but so important.

Joanna was sitting, a glass of soda water in her hand, surveying the bustling restaurant. I snuck up on her from behind, dropping a kiss on her cheek before climbing up onto a stool next to you.

"You look... fantastic," I said.

And she did. Joanna had been my best friend since forever. She'd sat next to me at lunch in first grade, and that was that. We were a pair. A perfect pair. She'd been the only one who could match my GPA, the only one that challenged me at cross country, and later at squash. We'd left business school together, degrees shining in our hands.

"I do, don't I?" she said with a grin.

I knew immediately something was afoot. "Tell me!"

"I'm pregnant."

A rush of something cold flooded my stomach. As much as Joanna had always been my competitor, she'd never been my rival. Far from instilling hatred, the competition between us had always brought us closer. I wasn't used to feeling envy. Not directed at her. I gulped.

"That's amazing," I managed to say, smile stretching out my skin.

She started to gabble about the plans she and her partner Lucas were making and I half-tuned in and half-tuned to my own feelings. This was ridiculous. So what? So Joanna had moved on a step without me. She was paired off and pregnant and I was broken up and... failing. No, not failing. I had to stop this. Had to stop measuring my life against someone else's.

I took her hand and squeezed it. "I'm truly happy for you," I said, making it true, banishing the jealousy.

"Good," she said. "Because it'd seriously suck if my baby's godmother wasn't excited."

And it took me a few minutes to get over that one, a sparkling glass pushed into my hand before I could stop it, talk of arrangements and details flying around.

"You're lucky to find me here," I said eventually when the news had been fully digested.

"I just stopped by on the off-chance," Joanna smiled, tossing her dark hair back over her shoulder. "I was heading this way anyway. But I guess I didn't see how late it was."

"We've had some excitement here," Addie put in. She'd appeared back behind the bar and was instructing Tom on how to make the perfect Tom Collins, though the poor guy definitely already knew.

"Like what?" Joanna said, turning back to me. She'd never approved of Addie. Oh, she'd hidden it well, but I knew, knew that Joanna hadn't warmed to her in the same way that I'd warmed to her boyfriend.

Quickly I filled her in on the dine and dash and when I was done, she was laughing.

"I can't believe you of all people chased a thief down the street," she said. "Your mom would have a fit if she saw that."

"Don't I know it."

"And what now?" She sipped her soda through a straw.

I shrugged. "Nothing, I guess. I mean, she's back there washing dishes to pay off her debt."

"Seriously? That's kind of old school."

"Her idea, backed up by Addie of all people."

Joanna sighed. "I guess it's easy to forget that some people don't have the advantages that we do."

That sounded judgmental and condescending. "She's a nice enough woman," I said.

Nice. Attractive was what I meant. She was attractive. Green-flecked eyes, hair in candy store colors.

"You're always trying to save people," Joanna said. "I didn't mean to sound preachy. I'm sorry. Maybe she just made a mistake. Maybe not. But is it really your job to protect her? To not call the police?"

"Benefit of the doubt."

Joanna sighed. "Did she look like she needed a decent meal?"

I nodded. A year ago, six months ago even, I'd be fighting this, telling Joanna how I'd made a great decision, enunciating the reasons why. Now though, I let it go. I wasn't sure myself why there was a thief washing dishes in my kitchen. Wasn't sure if I'd done the right thing at all.

"How's business?" Joanna asked, twirling her straw in her glass.

"About the same."

"Still losing money?"

"Not exactly losing, just not making." I told her about getting the accounts, about planning to go through them.

"Not a bad plan. Let me know if you need a second opinion."

The restaurant was really buzzing now, a line of two or three couples hovering by the door, waiting for a table. Addie had slipped away from the bar and was greeting customers, kissing those she knew on both cheeks, calling for drinks where necessary. This is what she was good at. The mingling, the social side of things.

"You need to stop this, Eleanor."

Joanna was watching me watching Addie and I knew what she meant but I pretended like I didn't because I didn't want to hear it.

"Stop what?"

"Stop trying to run a failing business enterprise with an ex-girlfriend who..." She trailed off.

"Who what?"

Joanna sighed. "Who isn't anywhere near good enough for you."

"Joanna!"

"Well, it's true. I kept my mouth firmly shut while you guys were dating, but now I can say what I like. And Addie isn't good enough for you. She's... flighty, unreliable, immature. None of those characteristics are things to treasure."

Tears were stinging my eyes, and irritated with myself I blinked them away. Joanna put her hand on my arm.

"It's tough, Eleanor. I get it. I know you made plans with her. But you have to let them go. You have to move on. And part of moving on means getting the hell out of this restaurant. Sell out, walk away, whatever you have to do. You can't keep coming in here every day and seeing her face. How can anyone move on if they're constantly confronted by their mistakes?"

I couldn't tell her. Couldn't tell my best friend in the world that I couldn't walk away because I couldn't stomach another failure. Maybe another day, maybe if she hadn't just told me that she was pregnant, that her life was moving forward. But not today.

"It's fine," I said, instead. "I'm dealing with it. And I'm just wrapping things up with the business. I told you, I'm going through the books. I won't be here much longer. Don't worry."

"I do worry about you," Joanna said. "I know you don't want me to, I know you don't need me to, but that's part of being a friend."

"I'll be fine," I said with far more certainty than I felt.

She sucked at her straw again until the glass gurgled. "You'd better be fine. I'm serious about the godmother thing. And I'd rather you acted as a role model as a happy and successful woman than as a basket case locked up in an asylum somewhere."

"I'm not getting locked up, Joanna."

"Better not," she said, jumping down from her bar stool. "And I've got to get out of here. Lucas has started getting all protective since the baby. I think I'm going to end up with one of those old people SOS buttons around my neck if I'm not careful."

I laughed at this and looped my arm through hers to walk her to the door.

"Look after yourself," she said as she kissed my cheek.

I was contemplating going home, getting a head start on those accounts, when the crash came.

It was loud enough that it silenced the entire restaurant, heads turning in confusion to the street-side windows and then the bar and finally to the kitchen door. Only when I saw others looking at the swing door did I realize myself that the commotion had come from the kitchen.

The kitchen. Mac. Crash. I groaned and started towards the door, already regretting my decision to keep the little thief here.

Chapter Nine

Mac

The shards of plates lay at my feet and I stared down helplessly at them. Tears pricked at my eyes.

"What the hell?"

The kitchen staff had taken a collective step back, like my clumsiness might be contagious. But Eleanor wasn't so superstitious. She stormed into the kitchen, her face red and flushed and even I started to tremble a little.

"What is this?"

She was close now and I could smell her perfume, light and floral. I could see a sheen on her nose where her makeup was wearing off and I swallowed and stuttered and couldn't say a thing.

"What happened?"

Again, nothing. I was waiting for it, waiting for the real anger to hit. Her eyes were dark, but she wasn't quite there yet. Another second or two. I could help it along if I could just speak. But all words deserted me. I really hadn't counted on this.

"Fingers like sausages," one of the cooks shouted over to a roar of laughter from the rest of the staff.

I felt my face blush bright red and now the words were starting to surface, there was something just on the tip of my tongue when she stared at me again and I was struck dumb. Again.

"Come with me."

She walked away and I followed, unable to stop myself. I took a last look at the broken pieces of plate on the floor. She hadn't even asked me to clean up.

Okay, here was what I'd expected, in as much as I'd expected anything. This plan wasn't exactly rocket science, but I'd had all of a half hour or so to come up with it. A half hour during which it had become rapidly clear that I wasn't going to be making a run for it with that damn gate locked.

The plan was that I'd drop the plates. Several. Make a big noise, create some chaos and confusion, and then... Well, that's where things got hazy. I told you this wasn't well thought out. My idea had been that one of two things would happen. Either I'd get the chance to run in the aforementioned chaos and confusion, or the boss would get so angry that she'd throw me out on my ear tired of dealing with my bullshit.

I'd obviously missed any opportunity to run. And now I'd missed the opportunity to get thrown out. Because though she looked irked, Eleanor didn't seem especially angry.

For the second time that day, I was off my game. I'd blamed Mia, thought that she'd thrown me off, made me too emotional to think properly. But I was starting to suspect that there might be more to it than that. In fact, I was starting to think that maybe this was about Eleanor, not about Mia at all.

Which was probably why I followed her into that little office. Pure biology. Like a fox scenting prey. I just couldn't help myself. Stupid, idiotic. I needed to find my head in all of this, needed to start thinking straight.

"Was it deliberate?"

I shrugged and she sighed.

"Sit down. Drink?"

She pulled a couple of water bottles from a shelf and I sat on a rickety chair in front of a rickety desk and wondered where the hell this was going. The hair on the back of my neck was prickling I needed out of here.

"Did you need the meal?"

"Yes." At least I was honest there. I had needed the meal. Maybe not in the way she meant, but I'd needed those few minutes of acting normal, being normal. Just a little time to be a woman sitting in a restaurant rather than a thief and a con artist and a scammer.

She sighed again and her chest rose in a way that was quite appealing. Appealing enough that I crossed my legs, trying to ignore the swelling feeling I had looking at her.

"Do you need a job?"

Jesus. This woman had a way of ripping my voice out of me and leaving me staring at her like a gaping fish. I couldn't even begin to process what she'd just said or why she'd said it or what it meant or anything else. So I just stared. That was all.

She got up and came around the desk, perching on the edge of it, close enough that I could touch her if I wanted to, which I did. But I didn't. Touch her, I mean.

"Mac, right?"

"Yes."

"I know nothing about your life and it would be arrogant of me to presume that I did," she said. "But I do know something about life in general."

"What's that then?" I was sounding sharper than I really wanted to. I didn't want to be lectured to, on the other hand, I did want to know where the hell this conversation was going.

"I know that sometimes people need a helping hand," she said simply. "Not a hand out or charity or anything like that. But a chance. Believe it or not, people have taken a chance on me in the past, and if they hadn't, I wouldn't be where I am now. So that's all I'm offering. A chance. If you want it."

A little burning feeling sparked inside me. "Let's get one thing straight, I don't need rescuing."

"I never said that you did," she said. "I'm simply offering you an opportunity to make some money in exchange for work. That's all."

I sniffed. I didn't need the job, obviously. I was just trying to think of a way to say no that would result in me walking out of the office, rather than her seeing me as ungrateful and finally calling the cops.

"I can promise that you'll get at least one full meal a day," she said. "All staff working a full shift do."

A full meal. I couldn't deny that a professionally cooked meal sounded good. But that wasn't what caught my attention.

Behind her, just off to one side, I could see the corner of what I knew was a safe. A safe. Money. Cash. Restaurants always had lots of cash. And this was a rich people restaurant, so plenty of wallets around, plenty of info that I could pick up from wealthy customers. Mrs. So-and-so off on holiday again, leaving her three-story town house unoccupied. Mr. What's-his-name brought his wife diamonds again. Knowledge is power, remember?

Now I'm no common thief. But there was an addendum to the knowledge is power rule that stated that knowledge is also valuable. Find the right market and some kinds of knowledge are worth more than you'd believe.

I couldn't say that I felt much like putting in a hard shift washing dishes or clearing tables. On the other hand, a few days of legitimate work could glean me enough ready cash and information that I'd be ready to pull another big job.

The gears in my head were turning and turning but my eyes were feasting on the woman on the desk in front of me. Look but don't touch, I reminded myself. She was nice to look at. A little eye candy never hurt anyone.

"No pressure." Her mouth tightened around the edges, the skin turning white.

She was getting irritated. I needed to answer soon. Was she really just a good Samaritan? It was rare in my world. Rare that someone gave something without wanting something in return. Which was why I didn't necessarily feel guilty about lying. Eleanor wanted something, just because I didn't know what it was yet didn't mean that it didn't exist.

"Are you serious?" I asked, not because I really doubted her but because I was stalling, trying to see the situation from every angle that I could. Trying to spot any traps.

"Deadly serious. A pay-check in return for an honest day's work."

Given the fact that I left my bag on the bed with all my hard-scammed cash inside and that there was a fifty-fifty chance that Mia was sharp enough to figure that out, I could probably use a pay-check. Even if it was only for a couple of days.

I nodded.

"Yes?"

"Yes," I said with a damn sight more certainty than I felt.

And she reached out to shake my hand, something that I hadn't planned on and that took me by surprise. I was no more prepared now for the flush that came over me when she touched me than I had been the first time. I was still trying to swallow down the heat when she smiled at me and I got shaky inside all over again.

"Welcome aboard," she said.

My hand gripped inside hers I had the sudden feeling that I was out of my depth here. What had I just agreed to?

Chapter Ten

Eleanor

N ice and quiet again. The morning sun was gleaming through the cleaned windows, the tiled floor was sparkling clean again. Even the coffee machine bubbled in the corner because I'd actually managed to remember to turn it on this time.

The restaurant was empty. And for once I felt like I'd made a good decision. Deciding to work on the books here, deciding that I wasn't going to let the restaurant pollute my home-life, that was smart. I might not be able to walk away right now, but I could at least draw a line in the sand.

Books and papers piled up in front of me and my laptop hummed on the next table. Figures were always so logical, so orderly, but today the numbers were swimming in front of my eyes.

I hadn't slept particularly well, which didn't help matters either. With a sigh, I got up and started making myself a coffee. Maybe it'd help.

I wasn't dumb. The problem was her. Mac. A stupid name if I've ever heard one. I wondered if it was even her real name. She could have told me anything. And there was a solid chance that I was never going to see her again.

Which was probably a good thing, given that I'd offered her a job. Why the hell had I done that? There was no rhyme or reason to it at all. Okay, so maybe she needed a little help. Okay, so maybe Joanna's words had been ringing in my ears. What she'd said about not being able to move on when you're constantly confronted by your mistakes had hit home. Okay, so maybe I'm a decent person, one willing to offer a hand to someone in need.

I wish all of that were true. I wish this was just a matter of me being sanctimonious and charitable. But it wasn't.

I spent long enough lying awake last night to have realized that it's not about any of that at all. That the only reason I offered Mac a job was because I was curious, because she'd caught my attention somehow in the middle of all of this and now I was in her web, getting slowly wrapped up in silk because I hadn't been smart enough to call the police and walk away.

The coffee machine hissed. There was something about her, something about her and I together. That warmth that had sparked when I took her arm, the way just the look of her eyes could calm the spiky anger inside me. I was attracted and repelled and I really didn't know which of these was the appropriate reaction. Because judging was hardly my major skill these days.

It was going to be fine. That's what I told myself as I took my coffee back to the books. It was going to be fine because Mac wasn't going to show. She'd got away with dining and dashing, no cops had been called, she'd be an idiot to show her face back at the scene of the crime. I hadn't known her long, but Mac didn't strike me as an idiot.

The thought of not seeing her made the sunlight gleam a little less brightly on the floor.

I WAS STARTING TO THINK about lunch, my stomach growling. The books had illuminated nothing. I was far from done, but in what I had examined everything looked just fine. Which I suppose I should have expected. Our projected profits were based on real numbers, after all, and the books just backed up the numbers that I'd already seen.

None of this came anywhere close to explaining why the damn restaurant wasn't turning a profit. I grabbed my mug and swilled a long drink of cold coffee, wrinkling my nose in distaste as I swallowed.

Rattling came from the kitchen, then the sound of a door banging. The place was about to wake up.

"Who's an early bird then?"

Addie appeared outlined in the door, her blonde hair glowing in the sun so that she looked angelic. Angelic and successful, a half dozen shopping bags looped over her arms. Even from here I could make out the designer logos. I shook my head a little. It was an interest of hers that I'd never really got. I was happy to shop once a year and bulk buy, just to get things over with. In fact, I'd be happier in a damn uniform so I didn't need to think about clothes at all.

"Looks like you got an early start yourself," I said.

"Early bird gets the worm," Addie said. "Although in this case the worm happens to be a purse that I've had my eye on for a while."

"Along with a few other things."

"No point in having a new purse without an outfit to match it, is there?"

And I couldn't help but smile. There was an innocence about Addie at times, only when she was comfortable, only when she wasn't desperately trying to impress. It was part of what had attracted me to her in the first place. "Coffee?"

"Please."

I got up to work the machine while Addie dumped her bags and then slid onto the bench seat next to my spot.

"Find anything interesting in the books?" she asked.

"Not really."

"So maybe you are over-reacting?"

I placed a cup in front of her and re-took my seat, careful to keep a couple of inches between us. "Maybe," I allowed. "But I'm not done yet."

"In the mean time, you're happy to pay over what little profit we're making to a new... what exactly is this thief supposed to be? A dishwasher? General dog's body?"

"Mac will step in where needed," I said. "Besides, we need the help with the dishes, and a busboy wouldn't go amiss either."

There was a long silence where Addie sipped her coffee and I wondered just where all this had gone wrong. I knew the breaking point, of course, but there must have been clues earlier, things that I missed.

I was broken out of my daydreams by a warm hand on my arm.

"It doesn't have to be like this."

Addie had shifted closer to me, close enough that I could feel the heat of her next to me. "What doesn't?" I asked stupidly.

"This, us. We don't have to be like this. We were happy."

And she's closer now, her words whispered and memory stirs within me so that my skin starts to flush even though I don't want it to. "We were."

"So, let's not throw this away. Let's not throw us away. We had so much good, El. Why let it all go to waste just because of one stupid little mistake."

If she hadn't said the word little, I might have fallen for it. I might have gone back in time and let her get away with it. But that word, little, it stuck in my craw and I couldn't shake it.

"You slept with someone else, Addie."

"A mistake."

"You let me come home and catch you in our bed with someone else. That's not a mistake. And it's certainly not little."

She sighed, but her hand was still on my arm. "You're right. Maybe I was unhappy. Maybe things were moving a little too fast. You were so caught up in the idea of moving to a new house, getting married, I got scared."

I swallowed but nodded. Her dark eyes looked into mine and they were like pools of melted chocolate, soft and warm.

"I got scared and I was an idiot. And I'd do anything to change it. I didn't realize how much I wanted you, how much I wanted the life we'd planned together, until you were gone, El. I'm so sorry. I know saying sorry doesn't begin to cover what I've done, but it doesn't begin to cover what I feel either. El, please, forgive me."

I didn't think she'd ever been so honest with me before. This was a side of Addie that I'd only caught glimpses of. The part that was vulnerable, not the normal brash, loud exterior. The restaurant was silent, I really didn't know what to say or do. I didn't know what I wanted.

Her hand tightened on my arm, her warmth moved closer. Then her lips were on mine and for a moment I fell into the familiarity of them. The taste, the touch, that I knew so well, the movements that I could predict like clockwork.

A flash of red exploded in my head. I saw legs entangled, I saw the sheets that I'd so carefully chosen wrapped around sweaty bodies, I saw the book that I was half-way through on the nightstand, unfamiliar glasses on top of it.

"Stop."

I pulled away, yanked myself away.

"No, Addie. Just no."

A shudder passed over her, but then she just smiled. She got up, picked up her bags, then shrugged. "As you wish," was all she said.

And I knew in an instant that what I'd taken for honesty had been nothing of the sort. Addie was whistling as she went into the back to stow her shopping.

Chapter Eleven

Mac

I pulled my jacket closer around me. Almost time now. Huddled in the doorway of a building, bags at my feet, I had plenty of time to think. Time is important, for all kinds of reasons. Right now, it was important because there are certain scams that are easier to pull at certain times, like around opening, or, in this case, closing.

Taking the restaurant job was weighing on my mind. Not because it was necessarily a bad idea, but because I wasn't sure that I was making the right decisions. My head was muddled. Fucked up. And I knew exactly why.

Eleanor. I wanted to kiss that stupid look off her face, I wanted to tear those stupid, conservative clothes off her body, I wanted... My breath was coming faster now, blowing clouds of steam from my mouth.

Emotions make for bad decisions. I know this. Uncle Frank always says to think with your brain, not with your dick. And I was worried that right now I was thinking with, well, with parts of my anatomy that weren't my brain.

Because she just wouldn't leave me alone. Because curled up on the couch last night trying to sleep and forget about the stupid mistakes of the day, her face had kept popping into my head and I couldn't make it go away.

A crush.

Just what I needed.

I saw a couple come out of the store opposite. My cue. I picked up the bags at my feet and hurried across the street, running through the door just as the cashier was rounding the corner of the cash desk.

"I know, I know," I called out cheerfully. "Closing time. I'm so sorry, I busted my ass to get here. But traffic was awful, and... And this will really only take a minute."

The girl hesitated. Young, that was good. That meant inexperienced. Though this scam tended to work pretty well with any cashier at any chain store.

"Or... I could come back tomorrow," I said, slowing down as I approached the cash desk. "You must be in a rush to get home. Working retail is no joke, huh?"

And I got her right there. She grinned at me. "You're telling me," she said. She looked over at the door, then back at me. "What is it you need?"

"Just a few returns. Super fast."

She licked her lips, glanced at the door again, then nodded. "Sure thing, happy to help."

I pulled the bags up and deposited them on the counter. "Here we go. So sorry about this."

The cashier emptied the bags out, the resulting pile of clothes still with their tags pathetically small. "Your receipt, ma'am?"

"Is it not there?" I asked innocently. "Oh, I think I put it in my bag for safe-keeping, give me a second."

I began rummaging through my purse and out of the corner of my eye I saw her hand hesitate and then reach out for the first item on the pile. "I'll just get started on scanning these while you look," she said.

As I said, time is important. At any other time of the day, the girl might not have been in so much of a hurry, might not have started the return before she saw my receipt. A receipt I certainly didn't have, given that I'd shoplifted the clothes from a different branch of the same store earlier that day. I continued to go through my bag, sighing in exasperation now.

"You know, it must be in the car," I said. "Just give me a few minutes, I'll run get it for you."

And now the girl had a problem. She'd already started a return without a receipt, which was against protocol and could get her fired. Plus, it was a minute or two after closing time and she didn't want to wait or risk keeping the store open while I went to my car. So she had a choice to make.

I was already walking toward the door when she called out. "Ma'am, ma'am?"

"Yes?" I half-turned.

"It's fine, ma'am. I've already started the return. And these are obviously new and from our most current collection, don't worry about it."

I smiled and thanked her and went to stand back at the register, patient and quiet as she scanned through the rest of the stolen clothes.

The easiest thing would be not to show up at the restaurant. I mean, everything being equal, I'd come out ahead. I'd got my meal, there'd been no cops, I shouldn't push my luck. I should stay the hell away from the restaurant and from Eleanor Shepherd.

"Here we go, ma'am."

The cashier counted out a small wad of notes and several coins. I sighed. This was a small time scam, not the sort I was going to get rich at. The problem was that anything more expensive than thirty bucks or so and no one was going to take a return without a receipt.

"Thanks, and thanks for bending the rules," I said, with a wink.

"Not a problem. You have a nice evening."

The store spat me back out onto the cold of the street.

A few shifts at that restaurant, however, and I'd not only get cash in hand, but potentially cash or wallets or phones in my back pocket, alongside potentially useful info.

It was a risk. But then, isn't everything?

The soles of my sneakers were thin and I could feel the cold of the street creeping up through my feet. Money. It all came down to money.

I'd gone home the night before, trepidation in my stomach. And when I'd seen my bag still lying on the bed, Mia curled up next to it, I'd had a burst of hope. A little bubble that tasted of cotton candy. Maybe not this time. Maybe she'd not looked, or hadn't been thinking straight.

But the roll of cash inside was smaller and weaker and staring down at my junkie sister I'd tried so hard to hate her.

I couldn't though. I just couldn't.

The easiest thing in the world would be to run away. Just go. I had wits enough, skills enough, to support myself. Maybe get myself one of those nice office jobs, all stable and secure. Go into work every morning and ask about people's kids and know that at the end of the week there'd be a pay-check in my bank account.

Leave the debts. Leave the stealing. Leave Mia.

I couldn't though. I just couldn't.

Mia hadn't run. Fuck knows who my dad was, he could well have done a runner, though chances were that he didn't even know I existed. My mom though, she ran. She looked down at two daughters, one barely old enough to work, the other not even old enough to shave her legs, and decided that enough was enough. So she ran.

And Mia had that same choice too. She could have left me, could have stuck me in the foster system. But she didn't.

Which is why I couldn't run now. Which is why I needed to figure out a way to get us on track. Get Mia into rehab, get the creditors off our backs, and get us where we needed to be. Both of us with nice little office jobs and steady pay-checks and, hell, casserole dishes and toilet roll holders, and little blankets that live at the end of your bed even though your house is too well heated to need a blanket in bed.

I could go work with Frank. A couple of months in his employ and we'd never be in debt again. On the other hand, I'd never be free again. Because once you worked for Frank, you didn't leave. Not unless you got shot or banged up.

Or I could work a few shifts at the restaurant, see what showed up. I had nothing to lose, did I?

I shivered a little and walked faster. It was going to be a cold night. Might as well spend it in the warmth of a steaming kitchen with a full belly.

All I had to remember was to think with my brain, nothing else. Eleanor Shepherd was an attractive woman. She was also in a relationship with the blowsy blonde, which made her firmly off limits.

Actually, everything made her firmly off limits. The very fact that she could invade my head and make me think of her more often than I thought of anything else was a big red flag.

But as I turned toward the restaurant, my heart skipped a little at the thought of seeing her again.

Chapter Twelve

Eleanor

B y the time that the grey of evening was creeping in through the window, I'd spent the day with the restaurant's books.

Not to mention spending most of the day with Addie.

She swanned around the restaurant pretending that nothing was wrong. But I knew her better than that. The lightness in her tone could very easily become meanness, especially when she wasn't getting her way. And apparently she was no longer getting her way with me.

I wondered where the strength had come from to tell her no. It hadn't always been there, I was sure of that. Even at the beginning, just after I'd caught her in the arms of someone else, I'd looked for excuses, for justifications and reasons.

It had only been my pride that had kept me from going back. That maybe and the idea that something was just a little off. Joanna didn't like Addie, and that should be good enough reason for me to be wary.

I sighed and pushed away the open ledgers. The restaurant was going to be open at any minute, I needed to clear away. Plates were already clattering in the kitchen, voices calling out cheerfully to each other.

Mac hadn't shown up.

It was to be expected, I supposed. I was surprised only at how disappointed I felt. Disappointment wasn't a familiar emotion for me. And it definitely shouldn't be something that I felt over someone like Mac.

"Coffee?" Tom asked, waltzing in with his normal enthusiasm. Honestly, I didn't know how he did it. He always seemed to be so eager to be here, so happy to start work.

"No, thanks," I groaned. "If I have any more caffeine then there's a solid chance that my heart is going to beat out of my chest."

"That kind of day, huh?" he chuckled as he opened the shutters.

Tom had been with us since the beginning. A contact of Addie's, he'd come in and immediately set to making procedures and schedules for the restaurant that we hadn't even thought of. He'd been invaluable. And other than his pay-check, the only bonus he'd ever accept was a plate of brownies. 'My caloric Achilles heel,' he called them.

I wasn't entirely clear how much he knew or understood about Addie and I. But he had seemed kinder in the last few weeks, less gossipy, his tongue a little less sharp. So perhaps he knew everything.

"Definitely that kind of day," I said as he flipped the lock on the front door, though the sign still said closed. We had another half hour of calm before the real work started.

Tom was fiddling with the coffee machine and I was staring off into space trying to think through our cash problems when the bell over the door clanged.

"I'm sorry, we're closed," I heard Tom say on automatic.

But something made me look up.

And there she was.

A gust of cold air entered the restaurant with her. Her nose was pink-tipped with cold, matching her hair in an odd kind of way. She was wearing the same old sneakers, the same tank top, and denim shorts over thick pantyhose, the same leather jacket.

She looked more or less exactly as she had the first time she walked in here.

And my mouth dried up at the sight of her.

"Hey," she tilted her head up a little in greeting and I remembered who I was and where I was.

"You should use the back door at the beginning of your shift."

"Sure thing."

She walked closer, her hands looked raw and red from being outside without gloves and I felt a stirring of pity, a desire to hold her hands in my own until they warmed up.

"I just wanted to say thank you," she said quietly, as she approached my table. "I realize I probably didn't seem very grateful yesterday, and that I made a terrible first impression. But I do have some manners, I swear. It's..." She took a deep breath. "It's hard sometimes," she finished.

"What is?"

"Being me," she said, with a crooked smile. "And I don't always treat people the way I should. So I'm sorry, and thank you for giving me this opportunity."

Her little speech caught me off guard. "You're welcome."

She frowned at my table, covered in books. "What are you up to here?"

"Accounting."

"Aha."

I should have stopped there but I didn't. I didn't want her to walk away. I didn't want to lose this moment. Soon there'd be others here, business would be brisk, there'd be no quiet to talk. So I explained. "The restaurant hasn't been making the profits we predicted. I'm just trying to figure out why."

Something gleamed in her eyes. "Mind if I take a look?"

If she took a look? At the books? Seriously? She was already sliding onto the bench next to me and I had no idea what she thought she was doing. "I'm not sure this is a good idea."

She cocked an eyebrow. "And why's that?"

Because I've got an MBA and can't see an issue so what chance do you have of finding anything I wanted to say. But didn't. She was already looking over the numbers.

"Everything balances out?" she said. "Cash, checks, credit card receipts? Subtractions for orders and deliveries?"

"Yes," I said doubtfully.

She sniffed. "It's a scam then."

She was so close to me that I could smell her, almost taste her in the air. Just a few hours ago Addie had been sitting in that exact spot. Just a few hours ago, I'd kissed Addie in that same spot. Dimly, I registered Tom going through to the kitchen, and realized that Mac and I were alone.

"A scam?" I said, not taking the words in at all.

I was too busy looking at her profile, seeing the neat way her nose sloped down, the way her eyelashes curled out. Too busy biting my tongue, wanting more than anything else to touch her. I found myself leaning in, getting closer to her.

"Mmm, probably," she said.

Just at that moment, she turned and suddenly there was only an inch between us. Her eyes were looking into mine and I knew that all I had to do was move the tiniest distance. All I had to do was decide, to take action, to press my lips against those soft, pale pink lips, to...

But I didn't have to. She was moving, getting closer.

Electricity sparked between us, I swear I could see it glowing blue and excited as she neared. I couldn't move, I was completely in her power, just waiting for that first contact, for...

We both pulled back. As though we'd both realized at the same time what was about to happen and how foolish it would be. Blood rushed through my veins, flushing my cheeks. I took a deep breath and then another, and only then did I realize what Mac had been saying.

"A scam?"

She shrugged. Her face wasn't flushed. But her lips looked redder, more swollen. "I'd say yes," she said. "I mean look here."

She showed me what she was talking about, explained it to me, and it was all so simple, so sneaky, that I was astounded.

"So someone gets to the cash after receipts are printed but before the final count is done," she said. "Or I guess after the count is done, but that's a lot harder to pull off. Once the end of night count is finished then not many people have access to the money bag. So if it were me, I'd get my hands in the register." She paused for a second. "There are other ways to get the cash out, of course," she began.

But she didn't need to finish. It all came together.

There were technically four people that had access to the cash bag and to the register. Me, Addie, Kyla, our Australian waitress who worked weekends only, and Tom. Addie and I wouldn't be ripping ourselves off. The money problems were constant, not just limited to weekends, so it couldn't be Kyla. Which left one person.

And suddenly Tom's eagerness to get to work, his constant cheerfulness seemed a whole lot less like him just having a good attitude. And a whole lot more suspicious.

He was back behind the bar now, humming and wiping glasses. He looked so... not guilty.

"I don't know," I said, looking at Mac.

Why should I believe her? She hadn't exactly proven herself honest. And yet, and yet... It all made sense this way. I'd been through everything with a fine toothcomb. This was the only possible explanation that made any sense at all.

"Takes a thief to catch a thief," Mac said.

Her eyes glowed almost golden in the light and I almost fell into them again, the memory of our closeness stirring something in my stomach. Something that I really didn't need.

"I need to talk to Addie," I said.

I had to tear myself away from Mac. If I'd stayed, I would have done something stupid.

Chapter Thirteen

Mac

"Just grab an apron from back there."

The blonde guy, Tom was his name, I was pretty sure, seemed nice enough. Friendly but not too friendly. His innocent looking blue eyes smile with his mouth, and as much as I wanted to have an attitude, I found that I couldn't.

It was stupid, I know. But I didn't want to be this person, I didn't want to be the dishwasher, the busboy, the one that people pitied and felt charitable toward. I worked hard. Okay, okay, I get how that sounds. I worked hard ripping people off, but hey, it was hard work. I worked hard and thought that I deserved a little respect. Respect I was unlikely to get with an apron tied around my waist.

Still, stupid seemed to be the word of the day. The word of the last two days. Something about setting foot in the restaurant made me... stupid. There was no other word for it.

"Alright," Tom said when I'd tied the apron around my waist. "Get started in here washing the dishes from prep and unloading the dishwasher when necessary. Once tables need to be bussed, then I'll give you a shout. 'Kay?"

I nodded.

"Lost your tongue?" He grinned again and looked so much like a little boy that there was a half-smile on my face before I knew it.

"Sorry," I said. "And thanks."

"For...?"

"For pointing me in the right direction."

He put out his hand and grabbed mine to shake. "Name's Tom."

"Mac."

"Nice to meet you, Mac." He held on for a second, then let go. "Don't think much of dishwashing, huh?"

"Does anyone?"

He shrugged. "It's a start. And after you make a good start, well, you work your way up. Six months of this and you'll be waitstaff if you keep your head down. Then the tips start rolling in."

"Chance would be a fine thing," I said before I could stop myself. Chill on the attitude, the guy was just trying to be nice.

"I'll train you myself," he said with a grin. He rubbed his hand through his pale blonde hair and was about to say something or do something when Eleanor's voice called his name. "Boss calling. I'll catch you later."

Another flash of grin and he was gone.

Speaking of things that made me stupid. Even Eleanor's voice sent a thrill through my stomach. Jesus.

And what had that been about? Sitting on that bench next to her I'd felt it, like a magnetic force, pulling me towards her, begging me to kiss her. Something I couldn't repel, something I couldn't control. Had I ever felt like that before?

I got started, hands plunging into soapy water. I couldn't remember feelings so powerful before. And there was no reason to have them now. Other than the fact that Eleanor was an attractive woman. Long, lean, her muscles would be taut beneath her clothes, her skin soft, that dark hair would cascade down her back... And those lips... The soft pinkness of them...

Water splashed back and I hurriedly turned off the tap.

Being here was dangerous for me in so many ways. I was such an idiot for coming back.

The police could be called at any time.

Eleanor knew exactly what I was, though I wished she didn't, hoped that she hadn't quite put me into the 'habitual criminal' box. Though that's what I was, if I was going to be completely honest.

I was undeniably and inexplicably attracted to the woman who was supposed to be my boss and who had come within a hair of calling the cops on me.

Oh, and that woman already had a girlfriend, just to add a little plot twist.

How perfect was all of that?

I glanced over at the back door. It was open tonight, the grill pinned back. I could walk out whenever I liked. The skin on my hands already felt tight from the water. I looked down into the bubbles, the pearlescent sheen of them.

Enough was enough. Enough of this stupidity. Enough of this... whatever the hell it was that was going on here.

The potential rewards weren't worth the risk of being here. I scraped my hands dry on the front of my apron and was working on untying the strings behind me when Tom walked out of the office.

His bounce was gone. His eyes looked red-rimmed, his mouth a white line. He didn't look at me, didn't look at anyone. He took a black jacket off the coat hooks by the back door and walked out. Without looking back.

I paused, no longer intent on removing my apron. The kitchen had stilled, the place quieter than I'd ever heard it. And then Addie and Eleanor exited the office. Addie gave Eleanor a nod and then pushed out into the front of house. Eleanor faced us all.

"Tom has left us," she said simply. "He's been let go. Which means we're short handed tonight. I'll be pitching in and we're trying to get in touch with Kyla, in the meantime, give help where it's needed, please."

She looked around as though daring us to say anything. When we didn't she turned on her heel and followed Addie.

It didn't take a genius to work out what had happened. As the chatter of the kitchen swelled around me, I went back to washing the dishes. I wasn't going to leave the place in the lurch now, was I? Correction, I wasn't going to leave Eleanor in the lurch.

Tom had been fired, fired for stealing the restaurant's cash. And something struck me as terribly wrong about that. I couldn't quite put my finger on what it was. Except... except I tend to judge people well, it's part of what I do. And Tom was no thief, no scam artist. He didn't have the hardness in his eyes, he wasn't constantly calculating and looking for escape routes, he just didn't have... whatever it was it took to be someone like me.

"DO YOU HAVE A SECOND?"

Eleanor looked tired, exhausted. There were grey circles under her eyes and she was practically lying on her desk. She jumped when I spoke as though I'd woken her.

"Of course," she said, standing up and blinking.

I cleared my throat. I hadn't really planned this out properly. "I think you've made a mistake," I said, slowly. "Firing Tom, I mean. I don't think he's the one to blame for your cash problems."

She looked at me, eyes deep as the sea, the blue of them hypnotic. I could feel the exhaustion flowing from her, mixing with my own, making my muscles even more tired, my feet ache even more.

"I don't think that's any of your business," she said.

She was coming around the desk, heading for the door, I guessed. And I could smell her as she got closer, the spice of her perfume, the slight undertone of sweat after a long night of work. I put my hand out to stop her. There was no point saying anything if I wasn't going to do it right.

"Tom isn't the guy you're looking for," I pressed. "He's not sneaky enough, he's... I don't know. But it's not him."

Her hand shot out and grasped my wrist and I gasped. Not in pain, but in pure pleasure as her skin connected with mine.

"How about you let me worry about how to run my own restaurant?"

I swallowed. "But–"

"No buts." She was closer now. "You have no business being here, no business interfering, and certainly no business telling me what to do."

But I wasn't listening anymore. Tom was the last thing on my mind now. Her lips, those perfect, pale pink lips, were moving and I wasn't hearing what they were saying I could only look in wonder as I moved closer and closer to them.

Her eyes shone in blue and then clouded with something, lust, I hoped, desire. I glanced at her gaze once, to check that I wasn't imagining this, and then I didn't have to imagine anything at all.

The kiss was as warm and as soft as I had ever felt, the pulse in my neck, in my center, began to pound and I wanted to move my hands, to pull her closer to me, but I didn't dare.

"Eleanor!"

With a start, I leaped away. Addie was standing in the doorway, her cheeks red and her hair messed up. Her eyes flashed. Eleanor took a step back, away from the desk.

"Eleanor, I expected better of you," drawled Addie. "Kissing the help. Honestly."

She turned to me, a look of pure disdain on her face. "And as for you, thief. You're fired."

I hesitated, didn't move.

"You're fired," she repeated. "Get out of here."

Life came back to my legs and I pushed past her out into the kitchen and then out into the cold of the night.

What the hell had I just done?

Chapter Fourteen

Eleanor

What had I done?

I screwed my eyes tight closed in the darkness of my room and tried to forget it all.

Forget firing Tom, my right hand man, the one I'd trusted and adored.

Forget getting Mac fired, the one I'd brought on board, the one I'd wanted to save.

But most of all, forget kissing Mac. Forget the warm softness of her lips, forget the force that pulled me toward her, forget how perfect and wonderful it had all felt for a moment.

I'd fled. Left Addie as angry as she was, scooped up my bag, and walked straight out of the restaurant. I couldn't handle it, couldn't do it anymore. I needed time to think, and space. Lying in bed I had all the time and space in the world, but it didn't seem to be helping.

Deep breaths. Slow, deep breaths. I'm Eleanor Shepherd. I could handle this. I could handle everything. I just had to look at things logically, that was all.

"You can't trust your own judgment." I said the words aloud, like that might help.

Evidence: I'd screwed up with Addie, I'd screwed up with the restaurant. My judgment, therefore, was fallible.

And yet... And yet I'd known that there was something going on with the accounts, my judgment had told me that there was something wrong. It had taken Mac to point it out, Mac to prove me right. Regardless, my judgment had been on point. That one time.

Mac. I groaned and pressed my face into my pillow so that I could silently scream without waking the neighbors.

Mac.

There was some kind of magic going on there. That was the only explanation I could come up with, as illogical and bizarre as it sounded. Some sort of sorcery, some kind of enchantment or spell was drawing me to her.

"She's the last thing you need." Again, I said the words aloud.

Evidence: She's a thief. She dressed like she was seventeen. She... Christ. What a snob I'd turned out to be. She was a different class, had a different upbringing, was... just different. Was that really evidence?

Throw in the fact that she could well just be running some kind of con that I didn't understand, and I had enough to convince myself that this was not a kiss that I'd be following up on.

Really not. So why did I want to? Mac was the last thing I needed. But she was the thing I wanted.

I reached out, pulled my phone toward me, checked the time and texted Joanna. The phone vibrated in my hand a millisecond after I messaged.

"You shouldn't be on your phone in bed," I said, as I picked up.

"Seriously? And what are you doing? Painting the bathroom? Working on cold fission?"

I laughed. Joanna was my best friend for a million reasons, not least the fact that she could cheer me up no matter how bad I was feeling. "I'm in bed," I admitted. "Tough day."

"Spill it."

I told her everything and when I got to the part about kissing Mac she whistled.

"Not so fast," I said. "That's not the end."

"It's not?"

"Addie walked in."

Another whistle.

"And fired Mac on the spot."

There was a pause and the sound of a sigh, then Joanna said. "Alright, first thing's first. Tom."

"I did the right thing. On the off chance that I didn't, then I assume money problems will continue and I will have the chance to apologize to Tom and set things right."

"Good answer. Next, kissing Mac."

It was a game we'd played since we were small, breaking things down into manageable pieces, making things make sense. Joanna was the best sounding board that I knew.

"Okay, a harder one. Let me think. A bad decision."

"Why?"

"Because I've just got out of a long term relationship and I'm not ready for something else. I'm definitely not ready for something else with someone like Mac."

"Yet you say that you're drawn to her?"

"I feel that way."

"So maybe you should listen to your... I don't know. Your heart, your body, whatever it is that wants to make this decision for you."

Not a bad point. After all, if I couldn't trust my own judgment, then I had to trust something, right? Still though, the answer had to be a no.

"She's a criminal, she's an employee, and I was acting on impulse. The evidence weighs more to the negative than the positive."

"Ex-employee," Joanna said. "But fair enough. If it was a mistake, it was a mistake. That leads us to the third issue: firing Mac."

"I wasn't responsible for that, Addie did it." But I knew what Joanna was going to say even as I spoke, and I knew that she was right.

"It was still partially your fault. It takes two to kiss."

"And Mac didn't deserve to be fired because I've got a crazy ex," I finished. "I know, I know."

Joanna laughed. "That's the first time I've heard you refer to her like that. Addie, I mean, as a crazy ex."

I let out a breath. "Well, I guess she wasn't always the best and most sensible person for me to be with."

Another laugh. "There's hope for you yet. So, you know what you have to do?"

"I'm on it."

I said goodnight and hung up the phone. I closed my eyes, maybe I could sleep now.

I BANGED ON THE DOOR. What used to be my door. Because of course I'd had to leave Addie in our apartment. Getting her to move out had been a nightmare, despite the fact that my name was on the lease, in the end simply moving myself had been easier.

"What?"

She opened the door, face still rumpled with sleep. When she saw me, her eyes opened a little wider. "El."

"I need to talk to you for a second."

"Can't it wait until later?"

"Not really." This wasn't a conversation I wanted to have at the restaurant. Our lives were entwined enough with the place, with each other.

She stood back and I walked inside, the familiarity of it, the smell, the look, taking my breath away.

"Coffee?"

"No, thanks."

"So?" She leaned up against the breakfast bar that separated the kitchen from the large living room.

I took a deep breath. "Addie, I get why you were angry yesterday."

"Not angry, hurt." Her face was set in a frown.

"Fine, hurt. I understand. I screwed up, and I shouldn't have done what I did there, and I certainly shouldn't have let you see it. We're broken up, but there's no need for me to rub your face in it. I apologize, I was very much in the wrong."

Her face relaxed just a little bit. I'd started with the apology. But what was to come next wasn't going to be nice. I could feel it. Still, I had to do what was right.

"However, I think that you were in the wrong by firing Mac. She needs to have her job back."

"Never. She shouldn't have a job in the first place," Addie said. "She stole from us. You literally just got done firing someone for stealing from us, and now you're telling me that I should give a job to someone else who rips us off?"

I took another deep, calming breath. "She deserves a chance, just like everyone does. Besides, we're short staffed enough as it is, without firing anyone else."

"Perhaps."

"Definitely." She was starting to waver a bit. Time to throw in my trump card. "And if it makes the situation any better, there's nothing between Mac and I. It had been a rough day, I was upset after firing Tom, I just... I made a bad decision."

The mention of Tom made Addie stand up a little straighter. It must have affected her just as much as me, something that I might have forgotten.

"I'm... I'm sorry about Tom," I said. "I know he meant a lot to you, to me too."

She nodded, eyes wary. She looked like she was about to say something, but at the last moment she turned away. "Fine," she said, not looking at me.

"Fine?"

"Fine, you can give the girl her job back."

Easier than I'd thought. Maybe Addie was getting close to forgiving me after all, closer to letting us both move on. I hoped so, for both our sakes.

"Thank you," I said, quietly.

Chapter Fifteen

Mac

Isn't that how it always goes? One screw up and you're back where you started. I didn't know why I was hurt or surprised or even vaguely shocked by this.

I'd broken the rules. One moment of weakness, one electric kiss, and now I was back on my ass without even a paltry pay-check to show for it. Worse, I'd not just kissed the woman, I'd kissed someone else's woman. Something that even Uncle Frank knew was crossing the line. You don't mess with someone else's broad.

"Head's up," I shouted as I ducked under the metal rolling door.

I wasn't in the mood to get shot, and even though there were supposed to be cameras everywhere I didn't trust Frank to be tech savvy enough to keep them up and running. Besides, they'd almost certainly fallen off the back of a truck and were unreliable at best.

"Yo!"

It was a shout of warning and I slowed and stopped, looking around the warehouse until I saw a flash of movement. I'd recognize that battered leather jacket anywhere.

"It's me, Jess. Mac."

He stepped out from between containers and a grin split his face. "Nice to see you, kiddo."

I got a hug and I could feel the shape of the gun beneath his jacket. "Boss around?" I asked, trying to breathe in as little of Jess's overpowering cologne as possible.

"In the office," he said. "Want that I bring up some coffee?"

"That'd be nice."

I skipped off towards the stairs, rickety, iron, shaking with every step that I took. At the top of the flight was Frank's office. A room crammed so full of paperwork that it had to be a fire hazard. Not that burning the place down would matter, not a lot of the documents were genuine.

He was sitting behind his desk, feet up on the corner, cigar hanging from the side of his mouth, TV blaring on one wall and phone jammed to his ear. I hesitated.

Uncle Frank was a bad man. That had been made extremely clear to me when I was a kid, when Mia was sober enough to care about such things. And he undoubtedly was. However, he was also a kind man. He'd dropped twenty bucks in my pocket every time I saw him, always had a candy bar hidden around somewhere. The only reason he hadn't paid off our debts was because he and Mia had fought so hard about it he'd ended up disowning her. Not me though. No, me he had a soft spot for.

"Mac, Mac, Mac, get yourself in here!"

I couldn't help but smile. I pushed into the office and was swamped in a bear hug so tight I could hardly breathe. Technically, Frank was my half-uncle. My mother's half-brother. But he and I had the same tight jaw, the same green-flecked eyes. "Uncle Frank, I'm suffocating."

He pulled away and let me collapse on a chair. "What a pleasant surprise."

I rolled my eyes. "You called me, remember?"

"I did?" He put his cigar back in the corner of his mouth, then nodded. "Yeah, you're right. I did. How's business?"

I shrugged. I didn't exactly keep what I did from Frank, there was no point, he had a finger in pretty much every scam in town. But as long as I kept things on the down low, he didn't interfere. "Up and down," I said.

"Getting tougher to pull the small hustles," he said, leaning back in his chair. "When I was a boy there was cash there for the taking for anyone smart enough to take it. Nowadays, it's all about the security cameras and fingerprint locks and God knows what else."

"I get by," was all I said.

I should have known better than to be at Frank's beck and call. And generally I'd have done this over the phone, let him spin me a story and then turn down his offer of work. But he'd caught me at a low point, right after I'd walked out of the restaurant, right after that kiss, and I'd agreed to drop in and see him.

"You should be doing more than getting by at your age," he grumbled. "You should have a nice little nest egg put by, something to tide you over. You and that sister of yours." He paused, then added: "How is she?"

I ignored the question. Some things were best left alone. "What do you want, Frank?"

"I want to offer you an opportunity."

I should have said that I wasn't interested. But he was sitting up now, leaning forward and the promise of money was in his eyes. I swallowed and kept my mouth shut.

"All I need is a runner. You'll get a box, deliver the box to an address, collect a tip and off you go. Three, four packages a week."

"Why me?"

"You're my niece. I want to help you out." I glared at him and he relented. "You've got the right look, that bike messenger kind of look, makes you look innocent. And all my normal guys have got eyes on them right now. I need a new face." He sat up even straighter. "A grand per package. Minimum of three grand a week. What do you say?"

I didn't even want to know what was in the packages. Three thousand dollars a week. I could have Mia in rehab this time next month. Our debts paid off before the end of the year. The thought of so much money made my mouth water. I desperately wanted to say yes. Instead, I stood up.

"I'm just gonna pretend you didn't ask, Frank, if that's alright with you?"

His eyes softened for a second, he almost looked guilty, then he nodded. "Alright, kiddo. Just trying to help."

"I know, I know."

I gave him another hug and he told me not to be a stranger before I ducked back out of the warehouse and into the crisp cold of the day.

I'd done the right thing. But I hated myself for it, hated that I needed that money so bad I'd almost taken the job. And hated that I couldn't put my dubious morals aside for even a couple of weeks and just do what he'd asked of me.

No job, no money, and nothing but a memory of a tingling kiss with someone else's girlfriend to keep me warm. Life wasn't exactly looking up.

ELEANOR HAD THROWN me under the bus. That's what all this came down to. She'd let me be fired for something that had been just as much her fault as mine. I knew that life wasn't fair, but seriously? The woman who'd decided to give me a chance, the woman who'd just offered a helping hand, was willing to let me be fired because we'd both indulged in a kiss?

I should have known better than to trust her. Obviously. Maybe this was just a lesson.

That's what I was telling myself as I walked slowly along the banks of the dirty river trying to figure out how the hell I was going to make some quick cash. And then my phone rang.

It was a blocked number, not unusual. Most people I know use burner phones anyway, so it's not like I know most people's numbers.

"Yo." Never answer with your name. You need to be able to deny that it's you if necessary.

"Hello, I'm looking for Mac?" The voice was so smooth, the consonants so clipped and proper, that it could only belong to one person. The last person that I wanted to speak to. I should hang up.

"Eleanor."

"Ah, yes. It's you. Uh, this is a little awkward."

"You're telling me," I said, still not hanging up. "You can't fire me twice, so what exactly do you want here?"

"I want..." She sighed and tried again. "I'd like to offer you your job back if you'd like to take it."

"And why the hell would I want to come back?"

"You might not, and I'd completely understand. But just so you know, I have spoken to Addie. I told her that, um, that what she saw was a mistake on both our parts." A pause. A long pause. "It was, wasn't it? A mistake?"

"A big one."

"Right, so I told her that. That it wasn't something that would happen again. And that you weren't to blame and you shouldn't be fired."

"Right."

It could solve my immediate financial problems. But then I'd have to see Eleanor again. My heart thudded at the thought of seeing her. No, I couldn't do this. It was too risky. Having a crush was fine, having one on your boss, on someone else's girlfriend, was not fine.

"Addie over-reacts sometimes," Eleanor said, her voice a little quieter. "There's no reason you should know this, but she and I, uh, we used to be together. Since we split up, she's been a little... sensitive. So what she saw affected her on a personal level. Just so you understand."

Split up. Split up? "You're not together anymore?"

"No, not that it's any of your business."

A weight was lifted off me, and it felt like I was drifting down the path rather than walking. I couldn't help but smile. I hadn't broken a cardinal rule, I hadn't kissed someone else's girl. "None of my business," I agreed.

"So, will you come back to work?"

I really should have said no. I really should have taken myself out of danger. But I didn't. I couldn't. That same pull that Eleanor had over me physically seemed to work over the phone as well. Because I couldn't say no to her if I tried.

Chapter Sixteen

Mac

This was a stop-gap. A temporary measure. That was all. I had decided.

Mia had been gone when I got home. Not surprising since for once she had cash. She'd be buying, using, hanging out with the kind of douchbag friends that got her high. So I'd had time to lie alone in my bed and figure stuff out.

There was no use giving up. That would get me nowhere. And I didn't have any current plans for anything big. The apartment rental scam was a good one, solid with little chance of getting caught. But I'd need cash to pay for the rental, so I needed to earn first.

That meant working at the restaurant. Or that was my excuse. Plus, there was still the chance of something coming up, me learning something, money being thrown at me, whatever. I'd take whatever I could get.

As for Eleanor. Well, that was what it was. She was attractive, but getting anywhere close to involved with her would be a mistake. For the time being she was a means to an end, and I'd stay out of her way as much as possible.

I didn't like the way I lost my wits around her. The way she made me suddenly stupid.

"Here."

Kayla was the new head waitress. Blonde, Australian, pretty in her own way. But nowhere near as nice as Tom. She tossed me a rag.

"And what would you like me to do with this?" I'd be lucky to get through the shift without punching her.

"Wipe down the windows out front."

With a sigh, I pulled my jacket on and went to do as I was told.

Eleanor wasn't there when I'd walked in, which was probably for the best. I couldn't help the sinking feeling of disappointment though. What the hell was wrong with me?

Okay, okay, she had shown that she was somewhat trustworthy. At least she hadn't thrown me as far under the bus as I'd assumed. That didn't mean that there was a relationship here though, God forbid.

My hands were freezing as I wiped the panels of the restaurant windows. Smearing the special chalk paint that Tom and now Kayla used to write the specials on the glass. It was oddly satisfying, despite the heavy coldness in my fingers. Pane by pane I cleaned each little piece perfectly before moving on to the next.

See? This is why an office job was for me. Data entry. Something like that. Something logical and orderly, something where I had a set task. Even something boring. I didn't mind. Do the same thing day in, day out, get myself ahead. Maybe get a mortgage when the time was right.

It might sound boring to some, but believe me, I've had enough excitement for one lifetime. One day, one day I'd buy myself a cheap suit, I'd get CVs printed, I'd show a brand new certificate from... somewhere, something to prove I could do the job. And then I'd join the rat race.

The thought made me polish harder, my rag squeaking on the glass. I just had to get a little cash, just had to pay off the big debts, just had to get Mia somewhere safe where she'd be looked after. And then, then it was suburbia all the way for me, baby.

I wasn't regretting my decision to turn down Uncle Frank. I'd like to say he was trying to help out of the kindness of his heart, but the honest truth was that as much as he might love me, and he did care, he wanted me to work for him because it suited him. No one's kind for no reason. No one helps you for nothing. Even family. It's just the way the world works.

Which brought me back to Eleanor. What was she getting out of all this? Maybe it was just a sanctimonious feeling of doing good. Maybe she was... I don't know, a recovering alcoholic trying to make amends. No, scratch that, I'd seen her with a glass in her hand. If she was a recovering alcoholic, she was a terrible one. So...

A hand landed on my shoulder so hard my knees almost buckled. "Hey!" I yelped.

"It's you, isn't it?"

"What the fuck...?" I tried to turn, but the hand was so tight on my shoulder that I could barely move.

"Jennifer Leighton? Or should I call you Jen? Or is there another name that you'd prefer? I'm sure you've got a boatload of them."

The voice was cruel and hard and not at all like the soft, excited tones I'd heard less than a week ago. But I recognized it anyway. Shit. I closed my eyes for a second, trying to think fast. Nothing for it but to blag my way out. I stretched my shoulders and the hand let go, letting me turn around.

"I'm afraid there must be some mistake, ma'am," I said as nicely as I could. "I have no idea who Jennifer Leighton is."

The woman, Cassandra, that was her name, was scowling at me. Not even a trace of doubt on her face. She knew me and she knew that she knew me. I remembered the smile on her face as she saw the apartment for the first time, the grin she had when she handed me the deposit money. And inside I started to shake, my stomach rolling over and over.

"Bullshit. You think there are two women walking around with stupid pink hair like you? Think there are two jackets just like the one you're wearing?"

"It's a big city," I said. And then I let a little anger enter my voice. "I'm afraid I'm going to have to ask you to take your hands off me. Or I'm going to call the police."

"I'll call them myself," she said, hand gripping my arm tighter. "Maybe then I'll see my deposit money again, what do you think?"

"Ma'am..." But I'd run out of things to say.

Denying this was getting stupid. I racked my brains. Was there anything else I could offer her? Never admit to anything, that was another of Uncle Frank's rules. Once you admit, then you can't go back. But I was beginning to see little choice here. Sure, the police might buy my story and let me go, but they might not. And even if they did, I'd be sitting in a police station for the rest of the day and there'd be no question of me coming back to work. Fuck.

"Ma'am," I said again.

"Ma'am, let go of that woman."

I hadn't heard her coming, hadn't heard the sound of her footsteps or anything else. But suddenly Eleanor was there. And Cassandra's hand was loosening a little on my arm.

"This woman is a thief," Cassandra said.

"This woman is an employee of this restaurant," said Eleanor.

Now there was doubt in Cassandra's face. Now she was beginning to think that maybe her memory was playing tricks on her. "An employee?"

"Yes. Is there a problem here?"

Cassandra let go of me. She was studying me.

"This happens a lot," I told her. "Maybe I've got a doppelganger walking around?"

She scowled. "Highly unlikely."

Eleanor sighed. "Do you have any evidence, ma'am, that this woman has done anything to you at all?"

"Uh... no. No, I suppose not." Cassandra was stepping back. The futility of this was starting to dawn on her. She had no evidence and couldn't prove a thing. The only thing stopping her from walking was that she thought she recognized me. And even that recognition was starting to seem shaky.

"Then I suggest you leave, before this woman decides to press charges," said Eleanor.

Cassandra nodded, walked a couple of steps backward, still watching me. Then she turned and fled.

I grinned at Eleanor. "Thank you."

She raised an eyebrow at me. "Do I want to know what that was about?"

I almost lied, but couldn't bring myself to. "Probably not."

"I'll let you get on with things then," she said.

It was only a step to the entrance door, but Eleanor paused before she went inside. She had a look of such sadness on her face. Sadness or maybe stress, I didn't know her well enough to judge. Whatever it was, she obviously dreaded walking inside the place. I guessed I could understand that. Working with an ex had to be a nightmare.

I hesitated for a second. Don't get involved, stay out of her way. That's what I'd promised myself.

But then she'd stepped in for me, vouched for me.

As much as I was a loner, I'd never really considered the advantages that having a partner could have. Particularly a partner as conservative looking as Eleanor, as innocent and trustworthy.

That was part of it. The other part was the look on her face, the hold she had over me, the way she made me stupid every time I saw her.

"What do you do for fun?"

"Huh?" she turned around in confusion.

"What do you do for fun?"

"Nothing, read, I guess." She frowned. "Why?"

I took a teeny step forward. Just enough that I could start to feel that electricity. I was playing with fire here and I knew it. But she had just saved my ass from a tiresome encounter with the cops. And she did look sad.

"Come out with me tomorrow." It was an impulsive decision.

"Huh?" she said again.

"The restaurant's closed tomorrow. Come out with me. Let it be my way of saying thanks. For all this, for giving me a chance."

She hesitated.

"No funny business," I said. "Just for some fun. Trust me."

"Nothing illegal?" Amusement sparkled in her eyes.

"Nothing illegal," I promised. "Just some fun."

There was a long minute where she didn't speak where she was weighing up her options and I couldn't tell from her face what she was going to say. Then she smiled and it was like dawn breaking.

"Okay," she said. "Why not?"

Chapter Seventeen

Eleanor

God knows why I agreed to this. To any of it. Except I wanted to see her. I felt that I owed her something, I was ashamed of the way Addie had treated her. But mostly, I wanted to see her.

And when she came practically skipping over to me, I couldn't help but smile. That was the effect she had on me. I'm not stupid. I have an MBA. I'm really not dumb. I could see what was happening here, I just wasn't sure whether or not I wanted it to happen.

Strike that. I knew in my head that this shouldn't happen. That this was the last thing that should happen. That Mac was the very opposite of anyone I should ever fall for. I was her boss, I was still getting over Addie, there were a million reasons. And why would a girl like this be interested in me? What did I have to offer? Money, I supposed. It had to be a scam.

But her smile seemed so genuine.

"The fair, really?" I said as she reached me.

"Can you think of somewhere better to have fun?" She looped her arm in mine and started steering me toward the entrance.

"I can think of a dozen places," I said.

"Name one."

And I couldn't.

She insisted on paying, fishing notes out of the inside pocket of her battered leather jacket. A grey woolen hat was crammed on top of her hair, the only deference that I could see to the cold. I was wearing my ski underwear under my clothes. I never took chances.

"Come on!" She was grinning and pulling me inside where the rides creaked and the music jangled in my ears.

My skin tingled where she touched me. No. Just no. Whatever it is, you need to get over this, I told myself. This is not what you need. Mac would never settle down in a nice house in the suburbs, would never want kids and a career and all the other boring stuff. And that meant she wasn't the girl for me.

And yet... And yet we talked and laughed and she pulled at my hand and got me onto the Ferris Wheel and when I was back on the ground and breathless with the height of it and the closeness to her she took my hand.

"Let's play a game," I said.

The shooting galleries were close. But I needed her to let go of my hand. Because it felt too good, too much like a perfect fit. And that was what I didn't need. Because I knew that I was being conned, scammed, used somehow. Just my judgment was so screwed up that I couldn't tell how. And I was going to get hurt here.

"Okay," Mac said. "Here, this is a good one."

She led me to a booth that had balloons pinned to targets. I stepped up to take a turn, the man taking my money, but when I turned around Mac was no longer beside me. I'd already paid though, so I lifted the fake gun I was given to my arm and aimed.

The first shot went way to one side, so I compensated. Where was Mac? The man moved away from me, went to take someone else's money. And that's when I saw Mac. My finger was already tightening on the trigger and I couldn't stop the shot. I fired, and Mac's hand shot out and burst a balloon on the target.

Frowning, I shot again, and she did the same thing again. Then she ducked away as the man turned his attention back to me.

A few seconds later I was holding a pale green teddy bear and Mac was walking by my side.

"Was that really necessary? The cheating?"

"The games are fixed," Mac said. "The gun is warped, the bullets are chipped on one side. You can't shoot straight. So, yeah, the cheating was necessary if you wanted to win."

"And you've got no problem with that?"

"Cheating someone who's trying to cheat me? No. Why? Do you?"

I opened my mouth and then closed it again. She had a point, I supposed.

"There are rules in life," she said. "Even for people like me."

"People like you?"

"Scam artists, petty criminals. You know what I am."

"What kind of rules?"

"Depends on what kind of person you are, I suppose," she said. Her voice was close in my ear, we were of much the same height. "For me personally, I won't steal from those that can't afford to lose. I won't steal from friends, family. It's... I don't know. It's a matter of drawing a line somewhere. If you have no morals at all then you might as well kill the next person you see and be done with it. If you're going to have morals then you have to decide where that line is going to be, the one that you won't step over, the one that defines how 'good' you are, though the definition of good is subjective."

"You stole from my restaurant," I said.

"It's a classy place. And restaurants like yours take a certain amount of loss into account, right?"

"We do." I stopped. "Would you dine and dash from my restaurant now?"

"No, probably not. I know you now."

"So it's easier to steal from a faceless business."

"I don't steal from friends."

Those eyes, bright green flecks sparkling in the lights from the fair, they took my breath away. "We're friends?"

She was moving forwards, closer, those lips nearing mine again and I knew that I shouldn't give in, that I shouldn't do this. But I also knew that every cell of my body was screaming out for it to happen. Then she stopped. "We're friends," she said, moving back again.

Getting involved with someone like Mac could only mean trouble. On so many levels. So why was I so disappointed that she'd stepped back, that our lips hadn't brushed again?

"Teddy looks cold," Mac said. She took off her hat and then pulled it onto the teddy bear's head, covering his ears. "That's better."

I laughed. It looked ridiculous. And she looked so pleased with my laugh, that I laughed even more.

"Come on," Mac said. "We're supposed to be having fun here." She looked around and then pulled at my arm. "Haunted house, let's go."

I'd always hated things like that. Places where people jumped out at you, that were designed to shock, to surprise. I looked doubtfully up at the fake spiders dangling from webs. "I don't think so." My heart was beating harder than it should.

"It'll be fine," Mac said.

"No, let's do something else." My mouth was dry now. A stupid fear, but a fear nevertheless.

Mac took my arm. "It'll be fine. I'm here."

My heart started to slow a little. And I let myself be led into the haunted house.

"YOU CAN LEAVE ME HERE."

"No, come on, let me drive you to your door at least."

We were in my car. The least I could do after the afternoon we'd had was drive her home. Mac had said that she could take the bus, but I wasn't having it. Now she sighed.

"Okay, take a right down here."

It was a rough area, the kind of place where junkies lingered on street corners. Given what little Mac had told me about her life, I wasn't exactly surprised. I did dart a glance at her, wondering if she took anything. But nothing I'd seen about her suggested that she did. She was just down on her luck, that was all.

"Pull in over there," she said, pointing.

I pulled to the curb in front of a building that looked like a motel but that was obviously some kind of apartment building. My hands were starting to sweat. This was all such a weird situation, so unfamiliar to me, so unlike me.

"I, uh, I had a really good time," I said, surprised at the truth of it. I'd had a very enjoyable afternoon. I'd forgotten about the restaurant, about Addie, for hours at a time.

"Sometimes you need a little fun," Mac said.

She looked antsy, like she couldn't wait to get out of the car. But something told me that wasn't the case. She was uncomfortable because she wanted me out of here, didn't want me to see how miserable her life could be.

"I had fun," I said, gently.

I looked down at the steering wheel. Okay, time to put on my big girl pants here. Time to clear up some of this mess. Poor judgment or not, I was smart enough to know that communication was key to any kind of relationship.

"Mac, listen," I said, voice barely trembling. "I had a great time. You took me out of my comfort zone. And I like you, really like you. I, uh, I don't think I'm wrong in thinking that there are some... feelings here."

She looked at her hands and said nothing, but a pink flush appeared on her cheeks. Real or fake, she was doing a good job of showing me she cared.

"But I think we can both agree that anything more than friends would be a mistake."

I waited. When she looked up she was still flushed, and her eyes were sparkling. "You're probably right," she said.

I smiled. "Friends, then?"

"We seem like an unlikely couple," Mac said. But she was stretching out her hand. "Friends though." We shook on it.

"I'll see you tomorrow then."

"Tomorrow?"

"At work."

"Right."

She hesitated for the faintest second before opening the door and jumping out. I watched her stride across the waste-ground in front of her building until she disappeared into the stairwell.

I was half-way back to my place before I noticed the bear in the back-seat of the car, Mac's hat still covering his head.

Chapter Eighteen

Mac

I felt lighter than I'd been for a long time. I hadn't meant to ask Eleanor out, it had just sort of happened. But I was glad that it had. Even though we'd agreed that nothing should come of it. It's not like me to run away from things, I'd prefer to confront them head on. I don't do running, remember?

But as I climbed the stairs and neared the door to the apartment, a shadow started to fall over me. Something didn't feel right. You learn to trust your gut in a game like mine. My mouth tasted bitter. Something was off.

I went slowly, keeping to the inside edge of the terrace. The door was closed, locked. I slid the key in quietly and then all in one movement turned it and jammed my shoulder into the frame so that the door burst open.

No movement.

I stepped cautiously inside, heart in my throat.

And that's when I saw her.

She was lying half in, half out of the bathroom, one arm thrown up, one by her side. Her skin was the pale white and blue of the lifeless. My stomach dropped. I couldn't process this. I took a step. Another. And Mia's chest juddered as she took a breath.

Jesus Christ.

She wasn't. She wasn't.

It was like taking off a suit of armor.

Mia breathed. But she'd overdosed. Again. And if I didn't do something then... then she'd die. I knew how this went. This wasn't the first time I'd been here.

My hand went to my pocket, grabbed my phone. Then I stopped.

I wish that I was a better person. Wish that I didn't have the feelings that I had right then. My phone lay in my hand, palm sweaty, and I looked down at my sister. My dying sister.

Eleanor

Okay, maybe I should have let things go. The hat probably could have waited until the next day. But I thought of how cold it was, I thought of the holes in Mac's sneakers, and figured maybe she needed a little warmth in her life.

Navigating back to the decrepit apartment building wasn't too hard. Forcing myself to get out of the car was. The place didn't look safe. Hell, I didn't look like I fit in in the slightest. But I gripped the hat tight in my hand and got out anyway.

Picking my way through needles and trash and God knew what else I knew that I wasn't just doing this for Mac. I was doing it for me.

Because as I drove away from her my life got darker by a shade. Because whatever I said, whatever the logic in my brain demanded, I wanted to be with her, wanted to see her.

Which meant my stupid, wrecked judgment was making me do something foolish like chase into a crack-den apartment block to return a hat.

The stairs were best forgotten. I tried not to look where I placed my feet. Only when I got to the landing did I realize that I had no idea where Mac lived. Maybe there were name labels on the doors or something. I took a breath and kept on walking.

"In here!"

I followed Mac's voice without really thinking about how the hell she knew where I was. I sped up, stopping only when I got to the door.

"Hey."

She was biting a fingernail, phone in hand when she turned. She blanched. "What are you doing here?"

I held up her hat in response.

"Fuck. Where are they?" She pushed past me, looking out the door, then coming back in.

"Where are who? What—"

Which was when I saw her. A body lying on the ground.

My first thought wasn't a charitable one. What had Mac done now?

But then I saw the worry on her face, and heard the sound of sirens in the distance and saw a frail chest rising and needle marks on a pale arm and put all the pieces together. And then boots were pounding up the stairs and lights were flashing on the ceiling and everything was action.

Mac

"You don't have to do this," I said.

Eleanor stood a little closer. The smell of her almost overpowered the sting of hospital scent. "I know I don't."

"Then why...?"

She rolled her eyes at me and the move was so undignified, so not what I'd expected, that I laughed despite myself. Despite where we were. "Because we're friends. And because you've had a rough evening," she said.

"You drove me to the hospital, you stayed."

"And Mia is going to be just fine," Eleanor finished. "But for the time being you need some rest." She paused for a second, a thoughtful look on her face. "Here's an idea: why don't you come to mine?"

"Huh? No, no, I couldn't possibly." She'd already done too much. Already seen too much.

"Of course you could. There's a spare room. There's food in the fridge and a batch of brownies I made this morning. A hot bath, a good meal, a decent night's sleep. You'll feel like a new person in the morning."

How could I say no? Images of fluffy white towels and warm down comforters filled my mind and I caved. Gave in because I was tired, stressed, because goddammit I wanted to. And because Eleanor was there. Because she hadn't judged or said anything, because she'd stepped in and stuck around. And because she smelled good. Because I wasn't strong enough to say no.

Eleanor

She looked so small, so fragile. Wrapped in a blanket on my couch, hair still damp, smelling of bubble bath, she looked almost like a child.

"This isn't the first time?"

"No. It's happened before."

"And there's nothing..."

She took a bite from one of the thick sandwiches I'd made, chewed and swallowed. "No," she said finally. "State rehab is a joke. There's a place... a private place. I'm just trying..." She sighed, shook her head and took another bite of sandwich.

I understood. She was trying to get the money together. Going private was liable to cost a fortune.

"There's bills to pay," she said now. "Debts to pay off. Rent to pay. You know how it is. But we'll get there one day. I'll get the money together and then..."

And then maybe her sister would live to see another decade. My heart was cracking and breaking with sadness. I put down my empty plate and against my better judgment moved to the couch, sitting as close to Mac as I dared.

"Are you going to be alright?"

Her laugh was bitter. "I'll be fine. Always am."

I put my hand on her arm. She was holding back, this was a facade, I knew that. This tough girl image was a costume she put on to protect herself. "It's alright to be upset. It's alright to cry. You don't have to be strong in front of me."

This was greeted by silence. Until she turned and looked at me, pain burning in her eyes.

"Can I tell you something?" she said.

I nodded.

Mac

I told her because I had no choice. Because the darkness and the heaviness of what I almost did were pulling me down, were going to sink me. Because I had to tell someone. If I was that dangerous, that immoral and wrong and terrible, then someone needed to know. Someone needed to protect the world from me.

"When I found her," I said. "When I saw her lying there, I thought she was dead."

Eleanor's hand squeezed mine, but she said nothing.

"Then I realized she wasn't, and I got my phone and I was going to call the paramedics but then I didn't. I stopped."

I swallowed, breathed, took a moment.

"I didn't want her to be dead. I didn't. But just for that moment, just for a second, I thought how much easier it would be."

And I hated myself for it. Detested myself, made myself sick.

"It would be easier," Eleanor said softly. "Easier to walk away. To leave her to fade away with the drugs. There'd be no rehab to pay for, you'd have no responsibilities."

I nodded, tears streaming down my face. I didn't know when I'd started crying.

"We all have thoughts like that," said Eleanor, voice still gentle. "All of us. But it's not the thoughts that matter, is it? It's the deeds."

She handed me a tissue and I wiped my eyes.

"You didn't walk away, Mac. You stayed. You made the call. You saved her."

"But I almost didn't."

"Almost doesn't count for anything in this world," Eleanor said.

She was smiling a little, the light was catching in her dark hair, the line of her neck was smooth, the weight of her hand in mine was warm. And every fiber of me strained to move closer to her. Every atom wanted to pull in, wanted to touch her, to taste her. I stopped myself, almost shaking with the effort.

So she was the one that moved. She was the one that pressed her lips against mine. She was the one that made the stars explode and my heart thrum with steady desire.

Chapter Nineteen

Eleanor

I'd pulled away from the kiss. Ended it. But I couldn't stop myself from softly brushing my lips against Mac's just one more time before I sent her off to bed. The woman needed sleep. She didn't need complications from me.

And me, what did I need?

The answer had become painfully obvious and I was sick and tired of denying it. I needed Mac. Hell, I didn't even know her full name. I just knew that I needed her.

Somewhere between chasing her down and kissing her goodnight I'd fallen for her and I'd fallen hard. It was all very well trying to pretend that I hadn't, but I was exhausted with pretending that everything was fine. Exhausted with keeping up the pretense that the restaurant was a great investment, exhausted with keeping up the pretense that working with my ex was no big deal.

So exhausted that I barely glanced at the window of the bakery as I walked by. Even the solid beauty of that wedding cake couldn't distract me today.

I walked all the way to the restaurant, letting myself in through the front door. My little oasis of calm and quiet. No one would be in for hours yet. The perfect place to work. The perfect place to think.

Mac.

Her slim body wrapped in that blanket sitting on my couch, her green-flecked eyes, the angle of her shoulder, the sweep of her cheekbone. She was all I could think about. My mouth practically watered at the thought of her.

I pulled my laptop and a sheaf of papers out of my bag and settled down at a table.

She was still so wrong, of course. But maybe not as wrong as I'd imagined. Yes, I was still recovering from a break up, but you don't get to choose when you fall in love, do you?

Yes, she was still a thief, a scam artist, but she wasn't doing it for personal gain, she was trying to get herself out of a hole. Still bad, still criminal, but understandable at least. And she was working at the restaurant, so maybe she was going clear, maybe she really was trying and just needed a chance.

I flicked my laptop open and got up to turn on the coffee machine while the wifi connected.

Nothing had changed with Mac, yet everything had. And I knew, if I thought about it, what had pushed me over the edge.

I'd given her a chance. I'd seen some good in her. I'd used my judgment that I thought was so poor. And Mac had proven me right. Last night, seeing her with her sister, seeing the raw honesty in her eyes when she told me that she'd thought about not calling the paramedics, that's what sealed the deal.

We've all had those thoughts. What if I push that woman in front of the subway? What if I punch that man in the face? What if I just walk out the door without paying? What if I slip that scarf into my pocket?

We don't all act on them, and very few of us admit to them. There was a truth to Mac. A misguided, crooked version of the truth, but a truth nevertheless.

So I wanted her. Needed her. Whatever. I was charmed by her, wanted more, wanted to know where this was all going to go.

I had to admit, I'd had more fun at the fair than I'd imagined. Being with Mac was easy somehow, like we'd always known each other. Familiar.

The coffee machine was starting to bubble and the smell was heavenly. I was just about to pour a cup when a shadow darkened the door. The bell dinged and cold sunshine spilled across the floor.

The thing with Addie is that she always Enters a room. That's Enter with a capital E. There's no mistaking when Addie is there, whether there's an audience to notice her or not.

She whirlwinded in, shopping bags dangling from her hands, sunglasses pushed up onto her head, and my heart sank.

"You're in early," was all I said.

She grinned. "That designer bathroom store close to the apartment is closing down. I got some amazing bargains. Figured the toilets could do with a spruce up."

Always with the shopping. At least she spread her money around. I knew for a fact that there was a solid chance she wasn't going to turn her receipts in to get reimbursed from the company accounts. Addie is generous, I give her that.

"Alright, I guess. Want a coffee?"

"Just finished one. I'm going to unpack my goodies and get started."

"Please yourself."

She went off into the back and I took my cup back to the table, moving papers aside to place it safely down. And then I saw them.

There was another reason that Mac was a most unsuitable choice. There was no way that a girl like that was going to want to live the kind of life that I imagined for myself.

The stack of papers stared up at me accusingly. Each paper held the details of a house that I'd once imagined Addie and I could live in. A comfortable house in the suburbs with a lawn and a garage and room for kids and maybe even a dog.

This is what I'd have to give up for a girl like Mac.

I was holding the papers, gazing at a picture of a cute ranch style house with a towering oak tree out front, when Addie came back.

"Screw it, too much caffeine never killed anyone," she said, going over to the coffee machine.

Hurriedly, I pushed the bundle of house papers into my bag. I didn't need Addie seeing them. Didn't need her... What would she do? When I'd shown her the houses she'd smiled but had hardly been jumping up and down with excitement. I'd always had the feeling that she'd agreed to a house because it was what I wanted, though I was sure she'd love it when she moved. Now though, now she was just manipulative enough to pretend that she wanted a house, wanted us to move.

"I think you'll find that too much caffeine can kill someone," I said, pulling my laptop closer to me.

"Bullshit."

"It's a stimulant. I'm no expert, but I'm thinking it could do a number on your heart if you let it."

"Eh, I'll take my chances."

The coffee machine hissed and whirred and I opened up my email box. The accountant had sent the numbers for the month. I clicked on the file to download it.

I waited. Mac.

She'd be in to work today. I'd see her. And I hadn't decided yet what to do about it. At least I was sure that she liked me too. Well, sure that my advances would be welcomed. There was still the chance she was somehow scamming me, though the more time I spent with her, the less likely that seemed.

Maybe I just needed to ask her out to dinner. Maybe... I could bake her a cake, cook her dinner. Did I need to impress her? Probably not, my inner voice said. Probably the best thing to do was be myself, do what I normally did, which was eat dinner at home with soft music playing. She'd taken me to the fair, which seemed a very Mac thing to do. So now it was my turn, right?

My heart beat faster at the thought of asking her out. She'd asked first though. I could do this. If I wanted to see where this relationship was going, then I had to ask. I glanced down at the house papers bunched up in my bag.

I was going to ask her. As soon as I could get a minute alone with her. I zipped my bag closed so that I could no longer see the houses I'd considered so perfect.

The accountant's file opened and Addie frothed milk into her coffee. I scrolled down through the spreadsheet, then went back to the top and scrolled down again.

"Shit."

"What?" asked Addie.

But I didn't answer her. I was too busy staring at the numbers. They weren't right, I knew they weren't right. I went over the last week, the time after Tom was fired, the time when things should be picking up again. Except they weren't picking up.

Which meant I'd made a mistake. A huge one.

Tom hadn't been stealing at all.

Chapter Twenty

Mac

"I'm sorry."

Mia's lips were cracked and her face was still an uncomfortable shade of yellowish white that I didn't like. But she was sober enough, she could talk. Relief made me light as I perched on the side of her bed.

"I know," I said. I did know. I knew this was a sickness, not a choice. It had taken me a long time to get to this point, a point where I didn't blame Mia for her addiction. It had been a long journey, but one that was important.

"I'm going to try," she said.

"I know."

And we both knew that she wouldn't succeed. I squeezed her hand.

"It won't be long now," I told her. "That rehab place will be so great you won't want to leave. Another couple of months and maybe we can afford it." Again, a lie that we both wanted to believe but honestly couldn't.

She smiled with her cracked lips and I saw tears forming in her eyes.

"Mac, stop this. You don't owe me anything."

"I owe you everything."

She sighed. "Mac, we need to be honest here. With each other, if with no one else. This is my problem, my issue, I can't just keep dragging you down with me. You don't owe me a thing, babe. I promise you that. You can walk away right now with a clear conscience."

I closed my eyes for a second, trying to stop the tears prickling there. "Without you, I'd have been a foster kid. I'd have been in the system. And we've both been round the block enough to know what happens to kids like us in the system. You owed me nothing, you could have walked away after mom left. But you didn't. The same as I'm not about to walk now. We're in this together, Mia. You and me and no one else."

"Trust no one," Mia said in a fair imitation of Uncle Frank.

"Trust no one."

She laced her fingers in with mine. "Just you and me, huh?"

"What?" I could see the sparkle in her eye. The sparkle that was so often snuffed out nowadays.

"Oh, nothing." But her voice said it was certainly something.

"Mia, tell me or I swear I'll yank out a catheter or drain or whatever tube I can get my hands on."

"Just, well, if it's me and you, then who was the woman?"

"What woman?"

"Um, the one in our shithole of an apartment that looked like a dead ringer for Kate Middleton? Talk about the Princess and the Pauper."

"It's the Prince and the Pauper."

"Don't stall."

"You really remember someone there?" I asked, curious.

"Narcan is a hell of a thing," Mia said. "One minute I'm floating away with the fairies and almost dead, the next I'm stone cold sober. I don't remember much. Flashing lights, feeling like shit, but I do remember her. She was like... Like some weird kind of angel. At least she seemed that way."

I snorted. Angel, my ass. "That was Eleanor," I said.

"Aha." She paused, but I didn't fill in the blanks. "Just Eleanor?"

"My boss," I said, with a sigh.

But Mia knew me too well for that. Well enough to know that there was something more. Something that I'd desperately like not to be there and yet that I couldn't help but long for. I'd been blocking out last night's kiss all morning and doing a damn good job of it, focussing on Mia and nothing else. But now the memory came rushing back with a flood of warmth.

"You like her, huh?" Mia said.

I shrugged. "Maybe." Denying it was pointless, Mia knew the truth just from my face, but I wasn't ready to completely admit it yet.

"Then what's the problem?"

I snorted again. A lady-like habit. "What's the problem? What's not the problem? She's attractive, a business owner, my boss, rich, law-abiding, feel free to fill in the rest of the sentence with positive adjectives that could never describe me."

"Is she straight?" Trust Mia, cutting right to the chase.

"No," I said with another sigh. "That's one point in my favor, I suppose."

"Do you like her?"

Such a simple question. I responded to Eleanor in a way I didn't really understand. My body wanted her, but that wasn't an unusual reaction to a beautiful woman. There was something else there.

I'd had no intention of working at a restaurant, I'd had no intention of asking her to the fair, I'd had no intention of letting someone see how shitty my life really was. Yet somehow Eleanor had made me do all these things. There was something instinctive about her.

I wanted to see her, I wanted to sleep with her, I wanted to spend time with her. I couldn't even begin to think about not seeing her again, the pain of that. Did that mean that I liked her? I suppose it did.

Mia had grown impatient. "I don't need you to answer that," she said. "I know you like her. I can see it in your eyes. So go for it. Forget about all the things that are wrong, forget about the fact that she's your polar opposite, and take a chance on someone. Trust someone."

"That from the person who just told me to trust no one."

"I was quoting Frank, as you well know. And look how far trusting no one gets you. Mom, Frank, me, even you, we're hardly shining examples of humanity, are we? So maybe try things a little differently. Let someone in."

The truth was that Eleanor had never given me a reason not to trust her. When she walked into that apartment, when she saw Mia on the floor, she could have assumed the worst. But she didn't. She didn't walk away. She knew what I was yet she'd invited me into her home, into her business, she gave me the benefit of the doubt. She acted like... like she trusted me.

"There's no way Eleanor will be interested in a criminal," I said.

"So stop being a criminal."

I laughed.

"No," said Mia, putting her hand on top of mine. "I mean it. Go straight. Stop this bullshit. Stop stealing, stop scamming. Don't be like mom. Or me for that matter. You could do this if you put your mind to it."

"Really? Then how are we going to pay our debts? Get you to rehab?"

"You're always looking for fast answers, Mac. Maybe this time there isn't one. Maybe we just have to work, graft hard, make the money the real way. I don't know. Or maybe just you, maybe I'm not capable. But I do know that you are. If you wanted to, you could go straight for this woman, if that's what it takes."

I smiled a little. Mia always had such faith in me. I wished I could have the same faith in her. I knew that it wouldn't be long before she'd be itching for another hit, until she was back out on the street.

"Maybe I will," I said. "You know, I'm working at Eleanor's restaurant right now." I looked down at the comforter, almost embarrassed by my admission.

"That's fantastic, Mac. See? I knew you could do it."

I smiled back at her. Her face had hope for the first time in forever and I didn't want to take that away. Couldn't take it away. Maybe I could do this, just like she said. Maybe I could give up my squalid life and be worthy of someone like Eleanor. Maybe I could satiate this burning need inside that I had for the woman.

And I tried as hard as I could not to see the hospital bed, not to smell the antiseptic, not to hear the machines, and not to think about yet another medical bill added to our already overwhelming pile of debt.

Chapter Twenty One

Eleanor

I didn't know what to say. I hadn't been nervous like this since I was sixteen years old and asking my first crush to go to prom with me. Every time I saw Mac my hands started sweating, and yet I couldn't take my eyes off her.

"It's only dinner," I muttered to myself.

But it seemed like so much more than that. It was much more than that. It was an admission that I wanted more, an admission that I was ready to do this, that I was over Addie, that I was ready to test out my shaky judgment on someone else.

Which didn't make things any easier.

It was a slow night at the restaurant. Any restaurant owner will tell you that Tuesdays are the worst night of the week, and this was no exception. There was a steady trickle of customers, but no rush. I kept a corner table at the back, ostensibly getting some paperwork done but in reality waiting for Mac to be alone, waiting for my opportunity.

"You're here late." Addie sat down on one of the ridiculously fragile chairs.

"Getting the accounts done, keeping an eye on things," I said, without looking up from my laptop.

She sniffed so I looked at her. The restaurant was close to empty by now, though it wasn't even ten.

"You can get out of here, if you want?" I tried.

She grinned at me. "You don't mind?"

"Place is empty, feel free."

"It's just that Paul has this party and..."

I waved my hand. "Not a problem. Get on out of here."

To be fair to her, Addie did tend to spend the most time in the restaurant, working bar, chatting, closing up.

I waited until she was gone, until the last table had paid and Kayla had flipped the sign on the door. The tables were cleared and the cleaners would be in in the early morning. No reason to stick around.

"Off you go," I told Kayla. "Take an early night for once."

I wandered back in the kitchen where the staff were busy wiping down surfaces. Mac was there, her back to me, hands in soapy water. Again with the sweating hands. Christ. I took a deep breath. How should I go about this?

"Mac, can I have a word please?"

I made it sound as formal as possible. Too much so maybe, because she looked up in surprise, then shrugged, wiping her hands dry on an apron before pulling the apron off and following me into the office.

I closed the door.

"Yes?"

I cleared my throat. "I, uh, that is, I—"

And she was already closing the space between us.

In the end, I had to say nothing.

Mac

I had to try this. That was what Mia was right about. Whether I could go straight or not, it didn't really matter. What mattered was that if I didn't pursue this, if I didn't do what my body was telling me I needed to, then I was going to regret it.

I liked Eleanor.

I more than liked her.

And when she called me into the office I thought I was being reprimanded or fired or something else terrible. But as soon as she closed the door I knew. I knew from the look in her eyes, from the heat of her, from the way she stumbled over her words.

So I took the chance. I grabbed my courage in both hands and took the step towards her and cupped her face with my hands and kissed her.

Soft and smooth and endless the kiss sealed my fate. As soon as our lips touched I knew that I would not, could not escape this. I pulled her in to me, I felt her cheekbones under my thumbs, I wanted desperately to touch her, to have more, but I didn't dare. Not here, not now. My heart was already leaping and my body burning but...

But I didn't have to do anything.

Because Eleanor's hands were already moving. Her long fingers were already pulling my t-shirt from the waistband of my shorts, her palms were already skimming over my hips and my waist and then up further, further, fingertips slipping under my bra, finding the hardness there, pinching in a way that made me gasp with pleasure.

And then I was helping, sliding pantyhose and shorts down, kicking off sneakers that I'd forgotten I was wearing, letting Eleanor lift me and place me gently on the edge of the desk as I opened my legs to welcome her in. To welcome her home.

Naked and shaking and so overtaken with desire that I could do nothing except experience what was happening to me. She came so close that I could wrap my legs around her and still we kissed, still those lips found mine, that tongue explored me.

Her hand slid down, finding space somehow to move between us, until she was cupping me. And my wetness was running down the inside of my thighs already and I'd never been so ready for anything ever before.

I broke our kiss, pulling away, wanting to see her. Those dark blue eyes half-closed as she sucked in air over her teeth and slowly moved her fingers, feeling how ready I was for her, feeling what she had done to me.

And that was as long as I could keep my eyes open for. My lids slammed shut, every nerve ending tingling with lust as her fingers found the hot swollen center of me and began to move.

I don't know how long it lasted. Time had no meaning. Probably it was over all too soon. But for those few seconds, minutes, all I could feel was Eleanor's fingers moving and circling and touching me in ways I'd always needed to be touched but never realized.

And when the end came, when I cascaded over the edge into a sky full of stars, blood pumping and muscles clenching, she pulled me tight to her chest and I bit her shirt to stop myself crying out her name.

Eleanor

I held her shaking, quivering body in my arms and felt a rush of desire and tenderness. As she slowly came back down to earth, her hands snaked up and around my neck and she hopped down from the desk clad only in her t-shirt and bra and pulled me to her.

I shouldn't let this happen. The little voice in my head was telling me this was wrong. The wrong time, the wrong place. I shouldn't be doing this. Good girls, nice girls, didn't do things like this.

But Mac brushed my lips with hers and her deft fingers started unbuttoning my shirt and I ignored any semblance of propriety. How could this be wrong?

She found bare skin, her hands burning against me, fingers unhooking my bra until she could bend that blonde and pink head and take my nipple into her mouth and send currents of fire down my body.

I heard a groan and knew it had to come from my mouth but I had no control over it. I had no control of this at all. I just knew that it needed to happen, the same as sneezing or breathing or falling asleep, my body was screaming out for this.

There was a scratching noise as Mac pulled her head away from me and dragged a chair from against the wall. Her slim hands slid up my legs, lifting my skirt until her fingers were tugging at my underwear, pulling them down.

I wanted to protest. The little voice, the proper part of me, the lady-like part, wanted to shout no. But everything else in me was screaming yes, and I was so tired of being sensible. I hadn't quite lost myself. I put my hands around Mac's wrists.

Her green-flecked eyes looked into mine. "Trust me."

And that was all it took. I released her, nodded, let myself be pulled down onto the chair, my legs naturally falling apart as Mac pushed between them.

Her lips were soft and hot as the brushed against my inner thighs. I had no shame, no thought for anything other than what was about to happen. My entire being was consumed by desire for her. I had to physically clutch onto the seat of my chair, preventing myself from bucking my hips to meet her mouth.

When she finally reached me, when I felt the soft tickle of her breath against my wetness, I almost lost it, I almost toppled straight into ecstasy.

"Mac."

My voice was a ragged whisper, nothing more. But it was enough. She pulled me closer, slid me along the seat of the chair until her tongue was lapping against me and my fingers were tangled in her hair.

Everything else faded away. It was like we were in our own bubble, suspended above place, above time. My breath came faster, my pulse started to race, and I knew I was close, but I didn't push to get there faster, nor did I hold back. I just let it happen.

And when she finally pushed me past my limit, I disappeared into the clouds with sparkles exploding over my skin and nothing had ever felt so right, so perfect, so fitting before in my life.

Mac

It was a long time before we left that night.

We talked, we touched, we laughed. And we decided.

This was no one night stand. This was something real. Both of us could admit that. And as the restaurant faded into silence and everyone left, leaving just the two of us, it all seemed so perfect.

It was long after midnight before I finally stretched and groaned.

"Home time," Eleanor said.

Her hair was messy, just as I'd imagined, her lips swollen with kisses, her eyes heavy. She was the most beautiful thing I'd ever seen. She offered me her hand and pulled me up out of my chair.

"I don't want to leave you," I said on impulse.

She laughed. "Who said anything about leaving me? You're very welcome to come with me. But I'm far too old to be sleeping on the floor of my office."

So I let her lead me, let her take me home. To her home. Let her hold me as I fell asleep. And trusting someone, letting them in, was far easier than I'd supposed. Easier, and far, far more comfortable.

Chapter Twenty Two

Eleanor

MacKenzie. That was Mac's full name. And it only took me a little over three weeks to get it out of her.

She was dipping behind the bar now, empty glasses in hand, and I smiled to myself at my little corner table. The last three weeks had been almost a lifetime and yet had disappeared in a snap of my fingers.

Mia was home, that much I knew, though I hadn't seen her. Mac spent much of her time at my place, something that I was more comfortable with than I would have imagined. She worked at the restaurant, collected a pay-check. And if she disappeared for a few hours every now and again I knew better than to question where she'd been. Or what she'd been doing.

I wasn't going to fool myself. I didn't believe that Mac was an angel. Or maybe I did, a flawed angel. My flawed angel.

"A scotch on the rocks for the lady."

The little dimple in her cheek made my heart swell as she smiled and I caught her hand. "Thank you."

"It's only a drink," she said, raising an eyebrow.

But it wasn't only a drink. It was happiness. A happiness that I hadn't known was there, that I couldn't believe I'd ever considered denying myself.

She went back to clearing tables and I went back to my laptop and I wanted everything to be perfect. Maybe we'd go up north for the weekend. Spend our nights in each other's arms in a snow-bound cabin.

As soon as I got the restaurant figured out.

This week's numbers were no more promising than last week's, and I was beginning to think that I was losing my mind. That I was chasing something impossible, or so obvious that I couldn't see it.

"Still looking rough, huh?"

Addie slid into the seat next to me and gave me a sympathetic smile and I smiled back. She'd been... oddly understanding. She had to know by now that there was something going on between Mac and I, but there hadn't been any temper tantrums. She stayed as far away from Mac as she could, but that was getting harder now. We needed the help, and Mac was spending more and more time out on the restaurant floor.

"Still looking rough," I agreed.

"Still sure you're not over-reacting? That you're not projecting profits that just aren't there?"

I rubbed tired eyes with my hands. "I don't know," I admitted. I hated admitting weakness in front of Addie. There was always the chance that she was going to take advantage of it. But I was too tired of all this to care anymore.

She sat back, crossed her legs out in front of her. "El, there's something we need to talk about."

In an instant, my heart was in my mouth. What did we need to talk about? Those words never brought any good. And with Addie there was a whole long list of things that we should probably talk about but that I didn't have the energy to address. Like Mac, for one thing.

"There is?" I asked, cautiously.

"Tom."

Even his name made me feel a little nauseous inside. But she was right. He had been blamed for somehow getting hold of cash before it went to the bank and helping himself. Yet money had continued to disappear after he was fired. Albeit at a slightly slower rate. Which meant he couldn't be to blame.

"Right."

"I talked to him."

I turned my head to look at her fully. "You did?"

Facing a problem head on like that wasn't exactly Addie's modus operandi. She preferred to ignore things until they went away. The financial problems at the restaurant being a case in point.

"I did."

"And?"

"And he's willing to come back. At least part time. I think I charmed him."

"I don't doubt it."

It was times like this, when Addie's hair was piled up on top of her head, when her eyes were sparkling and she was smiling her generous smile that I remembered why I'd been so attracted to her. We'd had good times. Really good times. Which was why the break up had hit me so hard, I just hadn't seen it coming.

Even then, even after seeing her with someone else, I'd been tempted to take her back. It was Joanna that had talked me out of it. Joanna who, over long nights of tears, had forced me to step back and take a look at things and shown me just how manipulative Addie could be. Just how wrong for me she really was.

"I'll need to call him and apologize," I said. The firing had gone as well as something like that could be expected, I'd been calm and reasonable and explained that we'd had no choice and Tom had denied doing anything. But of course he had. The action had been the correct one though, I was sure of that.

"You will," Addie said. "But I think it would be good to have him back on board. Besides, I feel like he's kind of our good luck charm. He's been with us since the beginning and things seem strange without him."

"Yeah. I guess you're right."

Up behind the bar, Mac was chatting to a customer, handing over his bill and smiling.

"Listen, I don't want to make trouble in paradise," Addie said.

Here we go. It was going to start. I knew there had to be an underlying motive. I was immediately on my guard. "Then don't."

"Mac's been on the floor a lot recently."

And just like that I saw where this was going. And I couldn't blame her. Because every time Mac stood in front of that cash register I got a little flutter of nerves in my belly. I wanted to trust her, I truly did, but... But leopards don't change their spots, the little voice in the back of my head said.

"I don't want to hear this, Addie," I said.

She shrugged. "Fine, then don't. I'm just saying that there's always the chance that we were right from the start. Maybe Tom was to blame but we fired him just as Mac came on the scene, and she took up the mantel, so to speak. She took over where he left off, knowing that we'd never blame her because she wasn't here when the problem started."

"Then why bring Tom back at all?" I said, but her words were floating around in my brain and I couldn't un-hear them.

"Maybe he deserves a second chance, just like Mac did," Addie said, sarcasm dripping from her tongue.

"You're a big believer in second chances, huh?" I said before I could stop myself.

"If by that, you mean that I think you should have given me, us a second chance, then yes, damn right I am. How could you throw away six years, just like that?"

"Me? I'm not the one that threw anything away, Addie. That was all you. You decided six years were unimportant the second you invited someone else into our home, into our bed."

"I was lonely, El. Why can't you see that?"

"Lonely? How the hell were you lonely? We lived together, worked together, we were together constantly."

"But you weren't there. Your head, your attention, it was always somewhere else. You were thinking about the business, about the house we were going to buy, about anything but me. And you were pushing me into this perfect life that you planned, one that I wasn't ready for. So, yeah, maybe you're right, I was the one that screwed up. But you were screwing up long before me, you wouldn't listen to me, wouldn't hear that I didn't want the same things that you did. You just kept telling me that I'd love the suburbs when we moved, that I'd love having a lawn, love having a big house."

My stomach ached like I'd been punched, I felt winded. "Why did you never say this before?"

"I did, or I tried to. But you weren't listening. And after, well, you never really gave me the chance."

I felt cold all over. Was she right? Had all the signs been there and I ignored them? Talk about poor judgment. I swallowed.

"Anyway, you're going to get what you want," she said bitterly. "A chance to make your investment back and to get the hell out of here."

"What's that supposed to mean?"

She took a deep breath and blew it out, trying to calm herself, a move that I knew well. Another and then she rolled her shoulders.

"I didn't mean to argue with you," she said, more calmly. "This is good news, not bad. And it's part of the reason we probably need Tom back, we'll need the help."

"What?" I asked, moving forward a little in my seat.

"A big catering deal. Huge, in fact. And if we pull it off, there'll certainly be more."

I knew immediately what she was saying, but I didn't want to believe it. "No."

"Yes," she said with a grin. "A wedding. A big one. Rock this and we'll be in the market. You know what wedding planners are like. Get into one planner's books and then everyone wants you."

"How much?" I couldn't help but ask.

Addie bent over and whispered in my ear a number so large it made me gulp a breath in before I could move.

"There's more," she said, flashing a grin at me. "They want a cake."

A wedding cake. My chance. Images of fluffy white frosting and sugar flowers were already starting to dance around my head. Addie laughed and squeezed my hand and my heart sang.

Chapter Twenty Three

Mac

Thank God the restaurant closed once a damn week. As much as I enjoyed working with Eleanor, and that really was the draw here, I could definitely get sick of the smell of grease and the sight of dirty dishes. The restaurant trade, I'd decided, was not for me.

That didn't mean that I didn't have other options though, as Eleanor was slowly teaching me. To be fair, she was teaching me a lot. I'd never realized, for example, how natural a relationship could be. How, even if you barely knew someone in reality, it could feel as though you'd known them for forever.

Or to trust.

Yeah. There was that. I'm no idiot, I know my own failings. And a complete inability to trust another living soul was one of them. Could you really blame me? The last person I'd trusted had been Mia, and as much as I loved her, I knew the days of putting all my faith in her had to be gone.

At least for the time being.

Which was kind of why I needed to talk to Eleanor. Last night she'd been too tired, this morning she'd gone out for a run. And when I was in the shower she'd got started on the latest incarnation of the cake.

The cake had come to rule her life. And by default, mine too.

"How's it going," I said, cheerily.

"Good, I think," she said, watching the mixer as it carefully churned the batter.

"Got a second?"

She looked up and her eyes were china blue and beautiful. "Not right now, darling. I've got to get this right, the clients are coming for a taste test on Thursday. Catch me later, okay?"

I nodded and blew out a breath. Patience. I had to learn patience too. Apparently. "Yeah, sure, fine. I'm off out, I'll be back later, yeah?"

But she was already disappearing back into the mixer bowl, a worried frown on her face.

I closed the apartment door gently behind me. Eleanor's apartment door. Because obviously it was her apartment. The furniture was hers. The restaurant was hers. My job was technically hers, I suppose, since she could give or take it at will. My other boss was her ex-girlfriend.

It occurred to me, not for the first time, that there was an awful lot of Eleanor in our relationship. And I was beginning to wonder what exactly I brought to the table.

Not that I had a lot to bring, I suppose. I almost tripped on the last stair down and swore. Even the stairs were out to get me today.

"COFFEE?"

The studio was clean. Or as clean as it could get. No clothes on the floor, no dishes in the sink. More importantly, Mia's eyes were clear. I wasn't holding out too much hope. But for the time being she was either not using at all, or, more likely, was making sure that she was clean before I came to visit. Because I always warned her now.

This place had stopped being mine sometime in the last month and a half. It hadn't been a planned thing, it'd just happened.

"Coffee would be nice," I said, flopping down on the couch. "Like what you've done to the place."

"You mean cleaned?" Mia said with a grin. "Least I could do for a visit from my beloved sister."

"You know, I'm still paying half the rent."

"And this place is still half yours, whenever you need it," Mia said, pouring boiling water from a pan into a cup of instant coffee.

"Not what I meant. I just meant that you generally don't need to clean up for someone that pays to be here. I'm not exactly a guest."

"You're worth it," she said, bringing the coffee over. "And I did mean it. This place is here for you whenever you need somewhere to crash."

"Thanks." It meant strangely a lot, knowing that I had a bolt hole if I needed one. I cleared my throat. "So, uh, how is everything?"

Mia looked down into her cup and I felt the shame coming from her and this part of the conversation was so awkward, but I had to ask. Finally, she nodded.

"I'm still on the methadone," she said. "It's... doing the job."

"For now," I said.

She bit her lip but nodded anyway.

"That's what I wanted to talk to you about," I said. "I've got a plan."

"Does it involve Frank?" was her first question.

"No."

"Let's hear it then."

Look, I wasn't saying that I was going to go straight. Not yet, at least. But there were certain advantages to holding down a job. Ones that I either hadn't known or hadn't thought about. Things that might help. I rubbed my nose, thinking about where to begin.

"Okay, I'm getting a pay-check," I started. "Which means I'm eligible for debt consolidation."

"What's that when it's at home?"

"The details aren't important. Basically, they put all of your debts together into one big bill and then let you pay a percentage of your pay-check each week or month to pay the debts down."

"Sounds like just paying debts to me."

I let myself smile. "It is, but with the advantage of getting creditors, loan sharks, or whoever else off our asses. All the debt would be owned by one place and we'd have a plan to pay it off. As long as we keep to that plan, it should be fine."

Mia's face brightened a little. "Alright, I get it."

"Which would deal with a big part of our problem," I said. "The second part of the plan involves you." I pulled the brochure for the rehab center out of my top pocket, it was battered, the edges soft from being carried around.

"We can't afford it yet."

"We can if I pay in installments," I said. "As long as I pay a deposit."

"And where are you going to get a deposit?"

I paused here. Then reluctantly said: "I was thinking about asking Eleanor."

"Seriously?"

"Not as a loan or anything. I mean as, like, an advance on my pay-check maybe. I don't know. I just..."

I just wanted my problems dealt with. I wanted them gone or under control so that I could enjoy this new life that I was getting. I felt like I was pulling Eleanor down, and that wasn't what I wanted. Not at all.

"And what does Eleanor think about this grand plan of yours?" Mia asked, her eyes narrowing.

I thought back to the last week. Every time I'd tried to talk to Eleanor she'd been too busy, she'd put me off. She was consumed by this stupid wedding cake. I knew I shouldn't take it personally, but I did, I couldn't help it. But it did mean that Eleanor didn't know about the plan.

"I don't know," I said. "I haven't told her."

Mia sighed. "Mac, love, I know that I haven't been the best of role models for you. I mean, hell, how are you supposed to know what a healthy relationship looks like when you've never even seen one? It's not your fault. But, well, I think even you know that you have to be honest with a partner. In this case, not least because you want to borrow money from her."

"Not borrow, just an advance," I said, hating the way this all made me sound, like I wanted Eleanor only for her cash. "And anyway, she isn't necessary. I could always come up with something to get a down payment. One last job."

"Isn't that what they all say?" Mia said. "I don't doubt your ability to get the money, Mac. I don't doubt your ability to fall on your feet. Even though I still say that you don't owe me anything. But I worry about you and Eleanor. You're not trusting her, you're not telling her everything. And secrets breed more secrets. Trust me, I know."

"Don't be stupid, of course I trust her."

"Then why haven't you told her?"

"Because..."

But it all seemed like too much to explain. The fact that Eleanor was so busy, so focussed on something else. The fact that I could feel her pulling away from me and that I worried that it was because of me, whatever the evidence said. Because I wasn't pulling my weight, because Eleanor brought so much more to us than I did.

Mia reached out and took my hand, squeezing it a little. "You gotta work on this, kiddo. It's rough. Figuring out how to have a good relationship is important though. Get it wrong and you won't last a year."

A year. A year with Eleanor. It sounded like an eternity. It terrified me. And at the same time made my heart beat faster and my skin warm and I knew that I wanted this. I wanted Eleanor and I to work out.

"I'll talk to her later tonight," I told Mia. "I'll tell her the whole plan."

But when I got home, Eleanor was still in the kitchen, flour dusting her hair, frosting on her cheek and a look of such intense concentration in her eyes that I knew I couldn't interrupt.

I kissed her cheek gently and took myself off to bed.

I'd try again in the morning, I promised myself.

Chapter Twenty Four

Eleanor

"So, the top up of cash from the wedding catering will put us on an even keel," I said.

Addie was tilting back in her chair, a sure sign of boredom. But then, business had never really been her thing.

Okay, that wasn't fair. The restaurant had been her idea. Her dream. She'd put a lot of work into it. Well, a lot of shopping into it. But she'd found the people she'd needed, had designed menus, and the one thing that I never worried about was the food. The food, the atmosphere, those were Addie's responsibilities, and I had to be honest and say that she had always more than fulfilled her side of the bargain.

It was my side that was more of a problem.

Because I was in charge of the business, the finances. And for a long time, the mistakes had been on my end. Were still on my end. For right now.

I was giving up. That's what wasn't being said here, what I was avoiding mentioning in the hopes that intimating it would be enough. Of course, it wasn't. Addie was as sharp as a tack when she needed to be.

"An even keel," she echoed. "Meaning what exactly?"

"Balanced," I said. "Books looking good, the restaurant looking like a suitably profitable enterprise."

Her jaw stiffened. "So you can walk out."

I took a breath. I needed to calm myself. I'd decided, decided that this all really needed to be over. It wasn't fair on Mac to keep myself here, to keep being around Addie all the time. And it wasn't fair on me.

I wasn't losing, I told myself. My judgment had been proven sound enough, I'd seen good in Mac, had made good decisions there. I'd done well leaving Addie, though it hurt. And I wasn't going to lose too much with the restaurant.

I was being honest. The cash from the wedding would make the books look healthy and therefore mean that I could approach someone else to take over my investment. In all likelihood, the restaurant would do very well once wedding orders started coming in, as I was sure they would.

"I'm not walking out," I said. But I was, wasn't I?

To my surprise, Addie's face sank and her eyes filled with tears which she blinked furiously away. "No. No. I don't want this."

"It doesn't matter what you want," I said.

She looked up at me, tears streaking down her cheeks. "How come she gets a second chance and I don't?"

It was very clear who 'she' was. "I don't want to talk about this, Addie. We've been over and over it and we are done. There's no second chance, whether you like it or not. I'm sorry that it makes you unhappy, but I'm moving on. That's part of why I need to leave the restaurant." I put my hand on top of hers. "And I think you need to move on too."

She pulled her hand away from mine. "You're wrong. You're wrong about all of this," she spat. "About me, about the restaurant, about Mac, about everything."

"About Mac?" I asked, curious.

"Looked at the books carefully, have you?" she said. "Because I have. I might not be an accounting genius, but even I can see that the one day a week everything balances out is on Fridays."

Fridays. When Mac goes to her sister's. When I said we should spend a little time apart, because it can't be healthy for a couple to spend every second together. When Mac didn't work at the restaurant.

"Bullshit."

"Check it." Addie folded her arms across her chest.

I stared at her for a second before pulling out my laptop and going through the spreadsheets that I had with a rapidly sinking heart.

"I'm right, aren't I?" Addie said.

I didn't want her to be. But then I realized that I'd been waiting for this. I'd been waiting to have myself proved wrong, waiting for the other shoe to drop. Mac was just too perfect. Life with her was just too perfect. It had been too easy. So, of course, it had to be a scam.

"You might want to think about the wisdom of second chances," said Addie, standing up. "And who you hand them out to."

She walked away. But just before she got to the door, she turned.

"I'll be here for you when it all comes tumbling down," she said.

And I was cold all over and didn't know what to think about anything anymore.

"YOU CAN'T LIE TO ME. It's impossible."

Joanna sat across from me, our table littered with the usual assortment of appetizers. Since high school, when one of us had a problem we'd hit a restaurant called Lucky's that was mid way between our childhood homes, order every appetizer on the menu, and talk, fingers squeaky with grease.

"I didn't lie. I might have withheld the truth a little," I said, dipping a mozzarella stick into marinara.

She took a chicken nugget, taking in what I'd just told her.

With no choice left, I'd spilled everything. Talking to Addie had been the last straw. I was so torn between trusting myself and not trusting myself that the only thing I could do was ask for an outside opinion. And the only person I could ask was Joanna.

She was blooming, in that horribly stereotypical way that some pregnant women have, her cheeks flushed and pink, her hair thick and bouncy.

"The restaurant obviously has a problem," Joanna said, finally. "And I'd agree with Mac, with you, with whoever, that someone is stealing. From what you've said, and from what I know about you, that's the only way you could be losing money. No one keeps more careful accounts than you, Eleanor."

"But who?"

Joanna's cheeks puffed out and then she let out a breath. "Your guess is as good as mine. I mean, it could have been pretty much anyone, excepting yourself."

"But was it Mac?"

"That's the real question, isn't it?" She chewed down on a french fry. "What's your gut telling you?"

"My gut has proven itself an idiotic liar."

"No, Eleanor, you've proven yourself a poor listener."

"Meaning?"

"Meaning that I get it, I see what you're getting at. You think you made some bad decisions, with Addie, with the restaurant, you think that your gut's lying to you. But the truth is that you don't always listen. Can you honestly look me in the eye and tell me that you never doubted Addie for a second when you were together?"

I bit my lip, remembering all the times I'd seen Addie lean in close to talk to someone else, all the times she'd gone out partying alone because that wasn't a lifestyle I wanted, all the times I'd seen her flirt at the bar.

"Sometimes," I admitted.

"There you go. And can you honestly tell me that you never once thought that putting money into a business venture with a lover perhaps wasn't the wisest of ideas?"

I sighed and rubbed my eyes. "Of course I did. I just... dismissed the negativity. Because it was so important to Addie."

"Which is exactly my point. Your gut speaks the truth, you don't listen. So what is your gut saying about Mac? Do you really think she's stealing from you? From the restaurant? Pulling a scam on you?"

I closed my eyes, seeing the fragile profile of a sleeping Mac, seeing her crooked smile, feeling her touch on my skin. "No," I whispered. "No, I don't think she's stealing."

"There's your answer then, darling."

I looked across at her. How I envied her. It had never really occurred to me before. But Joanna had the life I wanted. A loving partner that was besotted with her, a high powered job that gave her financial security and challenged her intellect, a weekend house and a large apartment, everything that I'd ever desired. But I couldn't hate her for it. I could only wonder where I'd gone wrong, what decision I'd made that had forced me off track.

"I wish I had your life," I said.

Joanna grinned. "My life is perfect. For me. You need to find your own perfection. And it probably won't look exactly how you imagined it."

"It won't?"

She rubbed her stomach, a non-existent bulge. "I never dreamed of having kids," she said. "You know that. But now... I can't imagine not having one. Perfection is what you make it, not what you imagine it to be."

I nodded and signaled the waiter for the check. "I need to get out of here."

"You need to go and see Mac."

She was right. I'd been distracted. By the wedding cake, by the restaurant, by the idea that maybe Mac wasn't the kind of person I should be with. And Mac deserved better than that. She deserved all of me.

But when I got home, she wasn't there. I waited up. But as time ticked on and my yawns grew more frequent, I couldn't stay up any longer. I pulled on one of her t-shirts and climbed into bed, falling asleep to the smell of her.

Chapter Twenty Five

Mac

"Do you have any other units?"

I'd dressed well, for once. In fact, I'd raided one of Eleanor's closets and taken something from the very back, knowing she wouldn't miss one grey skirt-suit out of what looked like hundreds.

"There's the penthouse suite," the man said. "We generally reserve that for honeymooners, but..."

"But my boss is a very demanding client," I said with a smile and a wink. "I know, I know. Trust me, I have to work with the guy every day. Just about does my head in."

The young man grinned and I straightened a little, giving him a good view of my cleavage. "I guess we could take a look," he said. "It's all rented out the week after next, but I think we could squeeze in a two day stay next week."

I followed him to the elevator, making polite small talk and wishing that I was wearing sneakers instead of these awful heels.

I'd tried, I really had. But talking to Eleanor was impossible. She was in the kitchen with her cake, or she was at the restaurant with Addie. And every time I thought we might have a second to talk something else came up. A phone rang or... Or my nerve gave out.

Then I'd cashed my first couple of pay-checks and realized... It took money to make money. Yet another one of those rules of the world that work out so unfairly for those of us without a trust fund.

The apartment scam was a good one. As long as I set it up right, of course. It took a little pre-planning. This time more than others, since I'd decided to go big or go home. No mid-range short term vacation rental for me this time. No, I'd hit up a top class business trip rental place, the kind of place that rented furnished apartments for more money per night than I made in a month.

Okay, I'd had to print up some business cards, slip a guy I knew a couple of twenties to make a phone call as my demanding boss, and, of course, borrow the suit from Eleanor. But all in all, the plan was going better than expected. There was a potentially huge payout here, as long as I had the balls to follow through.

But if it was going so well, why did I feel so shitty about it?

"And here we go," the rental guy said. He flung open a large door and let me walk into the huge apartment beyond. The view across the city took my breath away. He nodded with satisfaction. "I'll let you have a look around. I just have a couple of emails I need to check."

I turned sharp eyes on him, but he was already starting to scroll through his phone, no sign that he'd noticed anything, no sign that he was planning any kind of set up.

So I wandered into the bedroom. Taking a seat on the very edge of the bed I looked out over the view and shook my head.

Eleanor could buy this whole place. Given different circumstances, this bed could be ours. A year from now, two, we could be in our own place. I could be coming home from the office every evening, we could have a lawn.

I laughed to myself, except for once in my life that goal didn't seem so impossible. It seemed just that little bit closer.

I could wake up next to Eleanor every morning, I could kiss her goodnight every evening. She... she made me happy. She made me comfortable. She made me feel safe. And here I was being a spoiled child because she was busy for a couple of weeks, because she was pouring all her attention into making a cake rather than spoiling me.

Jesus Christ.

With a blinding clarity I suddenly knew that I was fucking up here. Big time.

The apartment was perfect, the job was all set up, and yet... And yet what would I be risking? Just for the chance to get a handful of cash in a couple of days. Cash that I could get more safely and less stressfully by simply being honest with Eleanor.

I tried to imagine not being with her. But I couldn't. I couldn't even think about not seeing her, touching her, feeling her ever again. Because somewhere along the line, somewhere in between the admittedly great sex and her inexplicable obsession with a wedding cake, I'd fallen in love with her.

My legs were so shaky with the realization that I couldn't stand up.

This was all so stupid, so ridiculous. Mia was right. I needed to let someone in, I needed to trust someone. I had to stop being so bull-headed and stupid, thinking I could do everything by myself. Mia had thought she could handle life all alone after mom left, and look what had happened to her. Who could begrudge her her dreamy leaps into the arms of whatever drug she could get her hands on? I swallowed. Now or never.

"Thank you so much," I said, sweeping into the living room. The realtor looked up from his phone. "It looks perfect, but I'll obviously need to run things by the boss before I can commit to anything. I'll call you."

I was already at the door, opening it, not giving him the chance to argue.

"Ma'am—"

"I'll get back to you as soon as possible," I said, closing the door mid sentence.

And I was running even before I hit the stairs.

"MAC, I—"

"Thought I wasn't coming back?" I said, leaning against the doorframe. "I was thinking the same thing myself."

Her face paled. A cooked but undecorated cake sat on the countertop. She flashed a look at it. "I, uh, I owe you an apology. I've been distracted, I've..." She paused and frowned at me. "Isn't that my suit?"

I nodded. "Can we talk?"

She took a breath and I could see the fear on her face. But she quietly walked through to the living room without questioning me. I grabbed a couple of glasses and a bottle of wine from a shelf before I followed her. I might need the alcohol to get through this.

"You remember when we went to the fair?"

"I do."

I was busy uncorking the wine. Eleanor took the bottle from me, poured a little, gave her glass an experimental sniff that made her nose wrinkle in the most adorable way, then poured us both a measure.

Why was I doing this? Because you need to trust her, I reminded myself. Because I didn't want to risk losing her. Because the only way that this weird, mismatched, opposites-attract kind of relationship was ever going to work was if we communicated, if we opened up.

"Right before we went, before I asked you, I mean," I stumbled on. "You caught me in front of the restaurant, a woman was yelling at me. Do you remember?"

Eleanor nodded, sipping at her wine.

"The woman was a mark. I'd scammed her. Out of quite a bit of money, actually. She had every right to yell at me. You saved me. If you hadn't come along, she'd have called the police."

"I'd guessed as much."

My eyebrows shot up. "You had?"

"I'm not foolish enough to believe you're an angel, Mac. And whilst at the time I just thought it was a typical big city crazy lady kind of situation, the more thought I gave it, the more I realized that the woman was probably connected to something you did in the past."

"But..."

"But nothing. I said you deserved a second chance. I meant it."

"You've no idea whether I deserve a second chance or not."

"I don't?"

"You don't know what I've done. How can you judge whether or not I'm deserving of mercy, of understanding, if you don't have the slightest idea of the kinds of crimes I've committed."

She eyed me then, those deep blue eyes staring into my soul. For a moment I thought she might change her mind. My stomach was shaking. Surely she was about to throw me out, to realize that I could never be the person for her, that there was no way someone like her could love someone like me.

Love. Even saying it in my head made me sweat, made the fear that much worse. There were some things that I wasn't ready to admit out loud yet, and that was definitely one of them.

"You make a good point," she said eventually. "I have no idea what you've been up to." She sat back on the couch, cradling her glass in her hands. My pulse thrummed in my veins. "So why don't you tell me all about it?"

I closed my eyes, letting the blackness take over for a calming moment. At least she wasn't throwing me out. No, she was making me confess all my sins, making me put my crimes into words. Maybe that was worse.

No, it wasn't, I reminded myself. If I wanted to keep Eleanor, this was the price I was going to have to pay.

I took a deep breath and began.

Chapter Twenty Six

Eleanor

She showed up on my doorstep and she told me everything. I didn't doubt that. All I doubted was myself. And when she'd finished, she sat, looking drained and I couldn't think of anything to say. Couldn't think of words to convey how painful her story was, how much I'd ached as she told me. Because to say anything out of place would sound like pity, and if there was one thing that Mac would hate, it would be to be pitied.

"So that's it," she said after a few moments of silence. "That's pretty much the whole sordid story. So, uh, if..."

She trailed off, collected herself, blinked away the tears that were almost forming. Still I couldn't speak.

"If you, uh, if you don't want to have anything to do with me anymore, then I'll understand," she finished, quietly.

I had to be logical here. I had to think with my head, not with my heart. Or with both maybe, I'm not sure. I did know that I couldn't let only my heart decide.

I should have trusted her. I should have trusted my own judgment. From the beginning, I should have given her that second chance and stood by it, stood by my own decision. The one thing that was becoming abundantly clear here was that I needed to move the hell on.

So I'd had a run of bad decisions. So what? It happened to everyone, every businessman, every entrepreneur had his failures. I was no different. There was nothing wrong with failing. But there was everything wrong with getting so hooked up on it that you couldn't take another step forward.

"I guess I should go."

Mac's words stung me back to life and at last I found my tongue. "No, no, please don't."

"Don't?"

"I don't want you to go. I just..." I took a deep breath. She'd been honest with me, it was my turn. "I was just thinking about myself, about my own mistakes."

"Getting involved with me?"

I couldn't help but laugh. "No, not at all. In fact, getting involved with you is the best thing that's happened to me for a long time. I was thinking about other mistakes."

"Like what?"

So I told her. I spilled it all. About wanting a perfect life. The mistake I'd made in trying to jam Addie into my picture of perfection. About investing in the restaurant when I really should have known better than to mix business and pleasure. And about losing my touch, doubting my own judgment.

"And then," I finished. "When I finally had something amazing right under my nose, someone who was my equal in every way, I become so distracted by a stupid wedding cake that I almost lose you." I laughed but only so that I didn't cry.

We sat there together in silence. It was too much to process all at once, this laying out of our faults. We needed time to think, time to formulate what would happen next. It wasn't an uncomfortable silence, it buzzed with activity below the surface. But I'd almost finished my glass of wine by the time I knew what I wanted to ask next.

"I have no right to demand anything of you," I said slowly. "But I can't be involved with anything illegal. I accept your past and understand everything you've said about it. I know that you made decisions in bad circumstances and at the time they were the best decisions you could make."

"I wouldn't say I made the best decisions," Mac said. She was staring down into her wine, the light catching in her blonde and pink hair.

"What's done is done. What I need to know is that things are different now. You're different now. If we're going to be in this together then we need to..." I took a deep breath. "We need to trust each other and rely on each other. I am more than willing to help you. But you have to be willing to give up these..." I hesitated, I hardly knew the words for what I was talking about.

"I need to give up breaking the law," finished Mac. "I know that. I do. It's only a matter of time until I get caught. I'm not stupid, Eleanor. I've got other options, you've shown me that I have other options. But I won't accept your charity."

"I'm not offering charity."

Mac nodded. "Okay. I can accept that." She looked up, eyes glowing green and gold. "I can work hard, Eleanor. Don't doubt that. I might have lead a life of stealing and cheating, but you know what? Stealing and cheating is an awful lot of hard work compared to getting a damn job. I can go straight. I can do this."

"I know."

She blew out a breath, then looked at me again. "But I need something from you in return."

Part of me wanted to argue. The little voice in the back of my head was screaming at me. She wants something in return? Something other than a free place to live, all the support she could need, a job that she never had to interview for? I gritted my teeth and silenced the voice. Mac wasn't trying to take advantage of me. She wasn't scamming me. I had to believe in that. "Whatever you need," I said.

"I need you to trust in me," she said. "I know I don't deserve it. But please, please, trust me. And by extension, trust yourself. You didn't make a mistake in choosing me, Eleanor. I promise you that."

My heart beat hard, once, twice, three times. My mouth was dry, my palms wet. I took a deep breath before I answered.

"Yes. Yes. I trust you."

She stared at me long and hard for a second then smiled a smile so bright it lit up the entire apartment. I looked away, embarrassed at how happy such a simple act had made her. As though giving trust were ever simple. I pulled my laptop towards me.

"We'll get you set up with a debt consultant," I said, going into work mode. "I've got a feeling that some of your mother's debts can almost certainly be written off. But a decent consultant will help you with that and come up with an affordable payment plan for you." I was already searching through results. "As for Mia..." I paused here, not really sure what to say.

Mac reached into her pocket, pulled out a battered prospectus, the edges soft with wear. She hesitated for only a second before handing it to me.

"This is where she needs to go," she said. "It's expensive, but they've got the best success rates in the tri-state area. I've talked to them about a payment plan already and they're happy to accept that on the condition that I pay a deposit."

This was the concrete version of all her hopes and dreams. The brochure had been stared at, fantasized about, had seemed almost impossible and out of reach. I could see that just from looking at it. There was no decision to be made here.

"I'll call them on Monday morning," I said. "And put the deposit payment through as soon as I get the appropriate banking information."

"No charity," Mac said, stirring in her seat.

"I'll deduct fifteen percent from your pay until the debt's paid off."

"Fine," she said, with a nod.

I went back to searching for a debt consultant. But a hand appeared over my shoulder, slowly closing the laptop in front of me.

"Hey, I'm trying to help you here." But I was smiling.

"And I'm trying to thank you," said a husky voice in my ear.

I let myself be pulled backward, let her arms encircle me. Her fingers were so delicate, her touch fragile as though she were afraid she was going to break me. Slowly, she slid her hand between the buttons of my shirt. I groaned as she touched my skin.

With one hand I reached back, tried to touch her, but she gently moved my hand away. "Let me," she said.

Eager fingers rumpled my skirt, pulling it up over my knees, sliding in, inching inside my underwear, finding the wetness that was so suddenly there every time she looked at me.

My breath caught in my throat as she began to move, stroking me softly and slowly so that my pulse started to pound.

I was almost there, so quickly, so wonderfully. I bit my lip, trying not to call out, not wanting to disturb this perfect moment in time where I hovered so close to ecstasy.

I heard it just as I disappeared over that edge, just as the stars started to explode, just as my breath no longer filled my lungs and my nerves tingled with pleasure.

"I love you," Mac whispered.

Chapter Twenty Seven

Mac

I should have known better, that's really all I can say. Since when has life ever turned out perfect for me? More Uncle Frank wisdom: If something seems too good to be true, then it's a scam.

And my life with Eleanor certainly seemed too good to be true for a while there. What? Healthy communication and being open and honest with each other didn't make for a happy ever after? Whoever would have thought that? Just goes to show, life's no fairy tale.

It started at three twenty seven in the afternoon. The light was starting to turn orange and the weather forecast had promised snow. And I know it was three twenty seven because I checked. Eleanor was at a meeting, leaving just Addie and I at the restaurant preparing for opening time. Except Addie, as per usual, made any excuse not to be in my company.

This time we'd run out of bar napkins, so she'd rushed off to get some before we opened. Sometimes I thought that shopping was her only real skill. But I'd sighed and let her go, knowing that the kitchen staff would be there before long, not to mention Tom who was all forgiven and back on the roster. Nowhere near as friendly to me as he'd been on the first day though.

All of which is why, when the bell over the front door rang and a gasp of cold air blew into the restaurant, I checked the time before greeting whoever it was who'd just come in. It was too early to be Eleanor back, too soon for Addie unless she'd forgotten her wallet, and the rest of the staff should come in through the rear. Which meant...

"I'm sorry, we're closed," I said as I turned.

The door was just closing behind a red-cheeked young woman. She smiled at me and I smiled back automatically. Her hair was bundled under a wool hat, and her eyes sparkled with the cold. "I'm not a customer," she said, quickly.

"Oh." There was nothing more I could say. If she wasn't a customer, then who the hell was she?

"I'm just here to leave the deposit?" I frowned. "For the wedding?" she filled in.

"Ah." Yeah, this was hardly me at my most conversational. I was trying to figure out what was happening.

"Someone, Addie, I think, said it would be okay?" She took a hesitant step towards me. "She said to drop by any time around now." She glanced back towards the door. "I guess I could come back tomorrow or..."

"No, no," I said, finally grinning and making sense of the situation. "Not a problem. Addie's just stepped out, but you can leave the deposit with me, I'll make sure she gets it."

The woman was reaching into her purse, pulling out a brown envelope that unless I was wrong, and trust me, this was not the kind of thing I was ever wrong about, held a big wad of cash.

"I'm really sorry," the woman said, noting my look of concern. "My parents are from out of state and didn't want to hand you a strange check, they thought cash might be better. If it's a problem I can write you the check right now?"

I was calculating, trying to see the scam here. But as hard as I tried, I couldn't see an angle. She must be telling the truth. "Not a problem," I said. "Just you leave that with me."

She handed over the envelope and said her goodbyes and I was left wondering what the hell to do with all that money. Finally, after realizing that I didn't know the combination for the safe, I figured that in the cash till was the best place. So I opened up the register, lifted the tray, and stowed the envelope safely underneath.

And then I went on with my day.

Eleanor

"Eleanor, we need to talk."

Addie had my attention immediately. If only because she never used my full name. Not for as long as I could remember. Even when we first met, she'd shaken my hand and called me El. So I let her drag me into the office without too much protest.

"What is it, Addie?" Not too much protest, but that didn't mean that I had time for any of her petty dramas. "Not enough candles? Someone else from the kitchen quit?"

Her face was white and her eyes wide and even as I spoke I knew that something far more serious was going on.

"I just got off the phone with Jessica Carhart."

"Who?"

"The bride, for the wedding?"

My heart sank. "Jesus, they haven't canceled, have they?"

"No, no." Addie licked her lips. "Sit down," she said, as she practically collapsed into the desk chair.

"What?"

"She'd told me that she was going to be dropping the deposit by today," Addie said, not looking me in the eye, still pale. "Wanted to know if it was a problem to pay in cash."

"Two thousand dollars in cash?" I said, surprised.

"Two and a half thousand," said Addie. "I told her that was fine, to drop in anytime this afternoon and one of us would be here to take it."

"Okay."

"But no cash appeared. So I called her a little after seven or so, asking if there was any problem, hoping that they weren't changing their minds or anything."

"Okay," I said again. The story was proceeding unbelievably slowly, like Addie couldn't tear the words out of her mouth.

"She said that she dropped the deposit off this afternoon," Addie said.

"Then I'm sure it's around here somewhere, I—"

"It's not," Addie interrupted, her eyes wild and fierce. "I've checked the cash register, I've checked the safe. There's nothing. So I called the woman back, asked her who she'd given the money to."

"And?"

I knew what was coming, I just couldn't get my mind around it. There was only one reason that I'd be sitting here. Only one person that Addie would have pulled me into the office for, rather than making a scene on the floor. But I wasn't going to believe it. I wouldn't.

"Eleanor, I just want you to know that I looked everywhere. Everywhere. And when you're done in here, you can go look yourself. That money isn't here. At least not where it should be." She took a breath. "Okay, so, she said she handed the cash in a brown envelope to a girl behind the bar."

My head whirled. Please, please let it be Kayla. Please let it be one of the kitchen staff getting a drink or some ice. Please.

"A girl with blonde hair with pink tips. She was adamant. You're welcome to call her yourself to check."

My heart stopped. My breath stopped. My whole world was coming crashing down. "How?" I managed to croak.

"It's my fault. I went out. We needed napkins. I knew that Jessica was coming with the deposit, but I went out anyway. I left her here alone, Eleanor. Mac was the only damn person in this entire place when that money came in."

Now my breath was back, hyperventilating, breathing so hard that my vision was going grey around the edges.

No. Not Mac. Please, not Mac.

Addie was reaching across the table. "I'm sorry, I'm so sorry."

There had to be another explanation. There had to be something. My brain was steaming trying to come up with something. I needed to check for myself, I needed to talk to Mac, I needed... But my legs wouldn't move. My tongue wouldn't move.

Mac

I stood there frozen for what felt like hours. Half a step away from the cracked office door. I listened and prayed and cursed, willing Eleanor into action. Please, just say something, just say it wasn't me, it couldn't be me. Say you believe in me, say you trust me. Just a word.

I could go and check in the register myself. But I knew in my heart that the envelope wouldn't be there. Someone was stealing. Or someone was trying to set me up. It didn't matter in the end, did it?

It didn't matter because as hard as I willed it, as much as I wanted it, Eleanor didn't speak. Not a word. She had nothing to say in my defense.

And just like that, the sky cracked over my head and darkness fell over me. I turned on my heel and ran. Ran as fast as the wind.

Ran down the corridor.

Ran through the kitchen.

Ran straight out of the gated kitchen door. The same door that I should have run out of the very first time I was at the restaurant. The door that should have let me escape then.

I leaped down the two stairs and then my feet were pounding pavement.

I didn't look back.

Chapter Twenty Eight

Mac

"Got a quarter, sir?"

The suited man hurried away without looking at me and I settled back down into my miserable corner.

This, this is what it had come to. Staking out a corner asking for spare change and swiping the odd wallet. Not exactly a full day's work, but enough to keep me and Mia in coffee and cheap white bread.

Whatever cash I'd had saved before we ran was just about enough to pay for a motel room up front. Enough to keep a roof over our heads for the next couple of weeks. Enough, hopefully, to give me time to get things worked out.

A week ago I'd been showering in Eleanor's rain shower, my skin pink with warmth and soft with luxury soap. More importantly, I knew that Eleanor was waiting for me. Knew that when I was done I'd slip into a comfortable bed and the waiting arms of someone who knew me for what I was and didn't care. Someone who trusted me.

And now look at me.

"Spare change, sir?"

"Get a job."

He didn't look at me as he sneered the words, but it didn't matter. In fact, it was better that way. All the easier to slide his wallet out of the back pocket of his pants before he hurried away. Never, ever keep your wallet in the back pocket of your pants.

I shuffled through it, taking what little cash there was. The wallet itself, complete with ID and credit cards would go into the closest mailbox. The bank on the main credit card would take things from there. I had no use for cards. Not right now. There were some scams that I wasn't set up to run, and that was one.

Here's something that no one talks about: how the digital economy has impacted those of us who live in the grey areas of life. Think about it. Who carries cash anymore? You pay for your Starbucks with your phone, you flash your card at the local deli. People not carrying cash was a big problem for people like me. Luckier for people like Eleanor though, I supposed.

Eleanor.

That long wait outside her office. Just waiting for her to defend me, to say something to Addie. That heavy silence. I re-lived those moments again and again and again.

And then the running. The smile on Mia's face when I banged into the apartment. The scowl when she realized what was going on. But she said nothing, just helped me throw some stuff into a bag and ran with me. Because that's what families do apparently, they run together.

I had to run. Here's what a lot of people don't understand. You get caught in a cycle. You get stuck just as surely as being superglued to a tabletop. And once you're in that cycle, your life is over. Once you're part of a lifestyle, it doesn't matter what you do or who you know or anything else, there's no escape.

Living on the fringes, like me, there's still a chance. I haven't been dragged into the center yet, I'm not quite a lost cause, no matter how I might look. And nor is Mia, for that matter. Not through lack of trying though. The fastest way for either of us to be pulled into that center, to lose our fate, our autonomy, would be to go and work for Frank. We both know that, it's why we've avoided it for so long.

There's another way though. Getting time.

As the long wait outside Eleanor's office had ticked by I'd seen a countdown clock inside my head. A countdown to Eleanor or Addie picking up that phone. A countdown to them dialing the number. A countdown to when the police would arrive with their flashing blue lights and cold as ice handcuffs.

That was why I'd run in the end.

Because once I was caught, once there was a solid case against me, which I had no doubt there would be, once I was in the system... Well, my life would be lost.

I'd be in a hole that was almost impossible to climb up out of. More impossible because I was exhausted. Tired of thinking and worrying, tired of money being behind every decision I had to make, tired of being responsible.

Sleet began to streak down from the grey sky and I pulled my jacket closer around me, snuggling as tight as I could into the corner that I'd found.

I was cold. I'd lost feeling in my feet hours ago.

It hurt. All of this.

It hurt because I'd let her in. Because I'd let myself be vulnerable. Because, and this made me feel like a fool, because I'd trusted her. And she hadn't trusted me back.

What use was there in opening up, in letting someone into your life, if they weren't going to trust you?

I'm no idiot. I had nothing to do with that money being stolen, and frankly, had no idea who had. But I didn't steal from friends and family. An unbreakable rule. I'd told Eleanor that. I'd told her that I was getting clean, going straight, giving up the scams and stealing. I'd admitted to her as I'd admitted to no one else, that I wanted out of this life. And she'd chosen not to believe me.

"Any change, ma'am?"

An older lady darted her eyes towards me, then without ever looking me in the eye dived into her pocket before depositing a small handful of coins into my empty cup.

"Thank you," I called after her.

Eleanor.

No, I had to stop thinking about her. I had to move on.

So I was begging. So I was cold. So I was living in a motel. So what? I'd been through worse.

I needed a little time, a little space to plan, a little cash, which I was slowly getting.

And then I'd rise from the ashes. Just like a phoenix.

I'd start over, just as I'd done so many times before.

The difference this time was that I'd never had hope before. I'd never had the promise of things getting better. I'd never had something I wanted snatched from beneath my nose so quickly.

Somehow that made it all harder. I don't know why. It was like how I could forget about being hungry right up until I walked past a bakery and smelled fresh cookies. And thought about Eleanor, flour sprinkled in her hair, trying and trying again to get the wedding cake perfect.

"Spare change?"

I rattled the cup in front of another older woman, but this one ignored me.

I didn't care. I wouldn't let myself care. I could do this. I'd done it before. I was strong. I was independent. I would let no one stand between me and what I had to do. Needed to do.

The street was empty now, the light turning grey and the air getting colder. I pulled my jacket close and emptied the cup into my pocket before putting my hands under my armpits to warm my fingers. Time to be getting back.

I had enough to feed us.

It was a long walk back to the motel. No point begging in a poor area of town.

It was dark before I got there.

And the tears were frozen on my cheeks.

Chapter Twenty Nine

Eleanor

I folded my arms and nodded finally.

"We can still do it," I said. "The wedding. Even without the deposit. I'll push an extra 5% into the business account and that should cover it."

Anything was better than telling the happy couple that we'd lost their money.

That someone had stolen their money.

Addie was agreeing with me, calm and collected for once, looking oddly skinny without her usual accompaniment of shopping bags. "The reputation we'll get from doing the job well will make up for the extra investment," she said. "We'll do okay out of this."

She said that almost as if getting robbed was the best thing that could have happened to us.

I leaned back on my bench seat and closed my eyes. Wishing things were different. Wishing I wasn't sitting in the damn restaurant again. Wishing that I'd made better decisions.

I hadn't wanted it to be true. When Addie had told me I'd had a moment of frozen paralysis. And when that moment was over, when the warmth of how I felt about Mac took over and thawed me out, I'd fought Addie every step of the way.

I'd demanded the place be searched, I'd talked to Jessica Carhart myself.

But in the end, Mac had incriminated herself.

Because if she'd done nothing, if all this was a misunderstanding, if I'd been right in trusting her and trusting my own judgment, then why had she run away?

I knew she'd run away. I knew even before I knocked on the door of the horrific apartment she'd shared with her sister. Even before the building manager, a man in a sleeveless t-shirt pulled over a beer gut, told me they'd ditched out in the night without paying what was owed. Even before I boxed up the few things that Mac had left in my apartment and thrown them out with the rest of the garbage.

And I didn't know what was worse. Facing Addie and admitting that she had to be right. Facing myself in the mirror every morning knowing that I'd been taken for a ride, that my judgment had failed yet again. Or facing that empty pillow beside me in the morning.

I cried. I tried to do it at home, alone. But sometimes it happened on the street, a shock flood of tears that came out of nowhere when I saw a leather jacket or a bottle-blonde head.

Everything just seemed so broken. Shattered. And I didn't know how to put anything back together again. Or even if what I had could be repaired. I just stared at the shards of my life and wondered what fit where and how the hell anyone could break something so badly.

It hadn't been so bad after Addie. Maybe because I'd been angry with her, and that anger had fuelled me, kept me going.

I was all out of anger though. All I felt for Mac was emptiness and disappointment. And those didn't fuel anything.

"Here."

Addie slid a cup in front of me. Only when I opened my eyes did I realize that there were tears there, that my lids were heavy with them. I gulped, sniffed, blinked and then gave Addie a watery smile.

To her credit, she'd never said I told you so. She'd never crowed or boasted. In fact, she'd done everything possible to keep the theft under wraps. She'd even dissuaded me from calling the police. There was no point, she'd said. Mac wouldn't be caught, and even if she were, the money wouldn't be coming back. Why keep prying at an open wound, she'd said. And I'd agreed.

Since then, she'd stepped back. Been quieter, softer, nicer. More like the Addie that I'd loved. It was almost as if she were shy with me, that she didn't know how to talk to me or act around me. Like I'd suffered a great loss.

"El, you're better than this."

The words came out of nowhere. "Than what?"

"Than sitting around here feeling sorry for yourself," Addie said, pulling out a chair. "You're stronger than this, better than this. I know it and you know it both."

I shrugged. I didn't know it. Not deep inside where it counted. Maybe I was no better than this.

Addie sighed. Then she reached out and took my hands, both of mine in both of hers. "I'm sorry," she said.

"For what?"

"For everything. I'm sorry for hurting you. I'm sorry for you being hurt again by Mac. You deserve none of it."

"You never apologized."

"For that afternoon?"

I nodded, the flash memory of those legs entwined, of the hair sprayed out across a pillow. No, not *a* pillow. *My* pillow.

"Because I didn't know what to say," said Addie now. "I was embarrassed, afraid, ashamed. And I knew that no words would change what happened. Nothing would change the shitty decisions that I'd made. But I am honestly and truly sorry. It wasn't my intention to hurt you. Though it was inevitable, I suppose. I never wanted to though. I just needed…"

"A life of your own," I said, understanding now.

"Yes. A little something that was mine. Not ours. Something that I decided, not we decided." She paused. "It doesn't erase the fact that it was a shitty thing to do."

"No," I said. "It doesn't."

The coffee was warm and sweeter than I normally drank it. But good nevertheless. Addie pulled a sheaf of papers out of a folder she'd placed on the next table.

"I found these in the trash can in the office," she said, spinning the papers around to face me.

"Because they're trash," I said, looking down at the house brochures.

"No," Addie said. "No, they're not. This one, the one with the bonus room over the garage. You loved this one." She shifted the papers a little. "And this one, didn't we want to go and see this one?"

I looked at the ranch house and nodded. We'd planned to go visit it as soon as we could snatch the time away from the business.

"These aren't trash, El. They're dreams." She shuffled the brochures back into a pile, looking down at her hands. When she looked up again her eyes were fierce and dark. "Dreams I'd like to share again."

I blew out a breath. This wasn't something I could deal with now, it really wasn't.

"We were good together, El. You know we were. We had something and I blew it. Because I was immature, because I wasn't ready. Things are different now. I've seen what life is like without you, and I don't want that."

"Addie, I—"

"No," she said, clasping my hands in hers again. "Don't answer me now. I know it's too soon. I know you're hurting and aching and you don't know which way is up. I just wanted you to know that I'm here. When you're ready again. I'm here and ready and I want to try again. I honestly do."

I nodded. There was nothing else I could do, nothing I could say. We had been good together. For a while. Addie gave me a small smile then pushed her chair back and got up.

I was left staring at the house brochures.

Dreams. All dreams.

The ranch house was right on top, it's siding and cute little window shutters looking quaint and just slightly kitsch. A house that I could have made my own. That Addie and I could have made our own.

Except when I squinted my eyes, when I looked real hard, it wasn't Addie that I could see sat there on a rocker on the porch.

It was Mac.

Chapter Thirty

Mac

"You got what it takes, kiddo. I wouldn't be offering you the chance otherwise."

Uncle Frank's bulk looked odd, outlined against the window of the small motel room.

I didn't know why I called him. Other than because I thought someone should know where we were. I mean, if Mia and I ended up murdered in our cheap motel beds, at least someone should know our real names.

"Frank, the offer's appreciated."

He narrowed his eyes and looked around the chaotic and very small room. "The offer's necessary. You girls can't live like this. Whatever happened, happened. But I won't let you go starving. You're my nieces."

I hadn't told him what had happened. Just where we were. And he'd come rocking up like he was some kind of benevolent angel, telling Mia to go take a walk, and plunging right into an offer of a piece of one of his pies.

And I was seriously thinking about it.

I know, I know. There were a million reasons to say no. A million reasons why this was a stupid, risky, terrible idea.

Except I needed out of this. I couldn't do this. Couldn't live on the run, couldn't deal with scraping a living and always wanting more, never knowing where the next penny was coming from, always terrified of being recognized or arrested.

Which meant one last scam.

The tag-line of pretty much every heist movie in history.

But I meant it. One last big job. Something to get both Mia and I sorted. The debts paid off, rehab covered. And then I was walking, going straight, taking care of myself. Turning myself into the kind of woman that Eleanor had wanted me to be. The kind of woman that Eleanor had made me want to be.

And then? Well, I had no idea. I'd get a job. Settle down somewhere. Get a dog maybe. Or a cat. But I'd be safe. I'd know that there was money in the bank to cover an extra dozen eggs when I needed them. I'd know that my health insurance would cover the broken wrist that I'd get from hurrying down the icy drive on the way to work.

"Can I have some time to think about?"

I needed more than time to think. I needed a way of convincing Frank that this was a one time only deal. A way of making sure I didn't just spiral deeper and deeper into his world. It wasn't going to be easy. Once I was in, once I was a part of things, then Frank would have something to hold over me, something to persuade me into doing another job. More than that, Frank's accomplices would have something over me.

So I'd need to tread carefully.

I'd need to get intel on Frank that would allow me to have the upper hand. Something strong enough, juicy enough, that when the time came I'd be allowed to walk away and go live my life in Dayton or Toledo or Indiana or wherever else.

"Yeah," grunted Frank. "I'll give you to the end of the week."

"Thanks."

He nodded, then peeled a couple of bills of a stack he took from his pocket. "Take this, get yourselves a decent meal."

"We don't do handouts," I reminded him.

"Neither do I," he said, grinning a little. "Call it an early birthday present from your uncle." He straightened up his jacket, rolled his shoulders then gave me a nod. "Make sure you call me before the end of the week."

And he was gone.

The door clicked open again almost as soon as it had closed.

"I saw him leave," Mia said, throwing herself down on one of the beds.

Things were strained between her and Frank. They had been for a while. Frank didn't trust addicts, with good reason. Addicts tended to sell out anyone they could for the price of a fix. So he'd never talk business in front of Mia. I think he blamed her for her weakness, something that he couldn't understand.

"Yeah," was all I said.

She turned over and I saw the restless look in her eyes. The methadone wasn't cutting it. She'd be back to using soon, if she wasn't already. "Did he offer you a job?"

I nodded, splaying myself out on my own bed, head against the headboard.

"Which you're not going to take, right?"

I shrugged.

There was a long silence and I could feel Mia's eyes on me and I knew she was judging me. But so be it. I was making the decisions here. And this time, I thought I was doing the best thing. The only thing really. As long as I could persuade Frank to let me go after one job.

"No."

The word startled me, and Mia sat up on the bed.

"No," she said again.

"No what?"

"I won't let you do this."

I sighed. "Mia, you—"

"I get it, I don't have a choice. I don't get a say. Because I'm not helping. Because I'm a junkie and a dependent." She took a deep breath and her cheeks flushed. "But I'm still your older sister, Mac. And I won't let you do this."

I shook my head. "You have no choice."

"I do. You don't remember this, but I do. I'm old enough to remember mom, to remember that every job was her last one, to know that you're falling into the same wicked cycle that she did."

"It's not the same."

"It is the same."

Mia got up and came to sit beside me.

"It's the same, Mac," she said more gently. "And I won't let you do it. You have dreams. Get them. Forget about me, forget about everything else."

"I can't do that."

"Then at least stop looking for quick fixes. The job with Frank won't be a quick fix, I can promise you that. There's no such thing as one last job, one last haul before you quit this life for good. There's always a catch. Just like with mom. You can still escape, Mac."

"I can't."

"You can. You can start doing this properly. You can work for a living, you can be honest."

Just like I'd promised Eleanor I was going to do. I swallowed, my mouth dry at the thought of her. I could prove something. Not to Eleanor, she was gone. But I could prove it to myself. If I had the strength to.

"The cycle is perpetuating, Mac. There's no later. There's only now. If you want to change, you need to do it now. Just like you don't wait to start your diet until Monday, you don't wait to quit smoking until New Year's Day. The time for change is now, Mac."

I was shaking, physically shaking. From fear, from emotion, from... I didn't even know what. I just knew that even my insides were trembling, even my bones tremored.

"I can't do it," I whispered. "I can't, Mia."

"You can."

"No."

She looked down at me and then took my hand. She squeezed tight, almost breaking my bones, before she let my hand go. "Then I'll give you no choice."

I closed my eyes. I knew what she was going to say and I knew how hard it was for her to say it. I remembered standing over her body, remembered my fingers itching to call the paramedics, remembered that just for a moment I'd honestly considered not doing it. Considered letting her die. Because it would be easier. Not just for me, but for her too. Easier for her to slide away from life without the shadow of her addiction stalking her.

And I knew that what she was about to do was just as difficult. Knew that we didn't owe each other anything because whatever I'd done for Mia, she'd returned to me, and vice versa. And I felt her take a deep breath, heard the oxygen filling her lungs, because making a big decision like that, it leaves you breathless, struggling to get enough air to your brain as though you're drowning under the weight of what you're about to do.

I knew all this and still I closed my eyes and didn't give up. I didn't tell her I wouldn't take the job. I didn't tell her that I'd go straight. I didn't tell her that I'd get my shit together. I could have made things easier on her, but I chose not to.

Maybe because I needed her to say it. Maybe because I needed to have someone there to take some kind of responsibility for once.

"If you take the job, Mac," she said, her voice calm and even. "I'll go straight to the cops."

Chapter Thirty One

Eleanor

"I can't stop thinking about her."

The truth came spilling out and I didn't want it to, but Joanna was half-smiling.

"Thus explaining the fact that you're white as a sheet and look as if you haven't slept for a week."

"I'm not sure that I have," I said.

Joanna sighed and came to sit down on the couch beside me. "Darling, I can't make these decisions for you, I never even met the girl. But if she's got you feeling like this, then is there a chance that you've made a mistake here?"

"No."

"Bullshit."

"I don't make mistakes." It had been a joke since high school. Eleanor Shepherd didn't make mistakes. She just didn't. Except now I did. Obviously. At least I'd escaped Addie's clutches for the day. She'd been following me around like a love-lorn puppy for the last few days.

Joanna settled back and crossed her arms. "Can we be brutally honest here for a few minutes?" she asked.

"Always."

"No, not always. Even best friends have to lie to each other sometimes. Lies are what makes the world go around. A... a social lubricant. The truth hurts, that's why we use it so sparingly."

I rolled my eyes. "Fine."

"You get too wrapped up in what's expected of you, Eleanor. You always have." She held up a hand to stop me talking before I'd even started. "No, hear me out. You grew up with the perfect life. A picket-fenced house in a nice suburb with parents who loved each other and loved you. You went to the right schools, played the right sports, got the right grades, and made the right decisions. Because that was what was expected of you. You assumed that the life waiting for you was the same life that your parents had, that same suburban perfection."

"And what's so wrong with that?"

Joanna snorted. "Remember when I got my nose pierced?"

I nodded, though more than the actual piercing I remembered the mess of infection that had resulted from it.

"Or when I dyed my hair green? Or when I dated that guy... the one with the mohawk... Tony?"

"Sure. What of it?"

"Rebellion is important. Most of us go through it growing up." She crossed her legs. "Look at it this way, how do you know if you like tomatoes if you've never tasted one?" I shrugged. "Exactly. That's what rebellion is. It gives you a taste of something different. And even if you don't end up liking all of it, you incorporate bits of that rebellion back into your normal life. It stretches your boundaries. But you never had that. Or nearly never."

"Nearly never?" I frowned. I understood what she was getting at, it was the nearly never part I didn't get.

"You almost rebelled," Joanna said quietly. "Right before we were going to college. You told me that you wanted to go to culinary school, that you wanted to bake. It was what you loved and you couldn't imagine doing anything else. I almost, almost persuaded you to tell your mom. But then you chickened out."

I could remember that. Could remember the conversation in my own head when I convinced myself that culinary school was not a sound financial decision for my future. Convinced myself that I could bake cakes and brownies on the weekend. I blinked back sudden tears.

"There's nothing to stop you rebelling now," Joanna said. "Nothing to stop you going to culinary school, wearing black eyeliner, dating girls with pink hair."

And I felt light. The feeling came from nowhere. It was as if I'd needed permission. Or needed telling that I could do this. My heart beat a little faster. Because she was right, wasn't she? There was no one stopping me doing whatever the hell I liked now. If I wanted to bake, and I did, I longed for it, then why the hell not? There was money in the bank, I could support myself while I got set up.

If I wanted to date girls with pink hair, well then... Well then there was something stopping me. Wasn't there?

"Joanna, I... Mac."

She bit her lip and creased her brow. "I've been thinking about that," she said. "And I don't think your judgment is that bad."

"You don't?"

"No, you're smarter than that. You're more instinctual. I don't think you could have misjudged someone that badly. Think about it. Really think. Do you honestly think Mac did this?"

I'd done nothing but think about it. I closed my eyes now, willing new information to come to me. But it didn't. Mac had been there, Mac was a thief, and money had gone missing. It all added up. And she'd run away.

Okay, okay, she'd told me that she had standards. That she never stole from those that couldn't afford it. That she never stole from friends or family. I wanted to believe that, I truly did. I wanted it with all my heart. But I couldn't escape the fact that the wedding money was gone.

"I've tried thinking of this every way I can," I said. "It's what's keeping me up at night. But I can't put the pieces together any other way, Joanna. I can't."

"Really?"

She was looking at me through narrowed eyes like she'd worked out something that I hadn't. And I felt a little bounce of hope inside my stomach. I quickly quashed it. I couldn't afford hope. I couldn't. There were no other explanations here.

"Look, with Tom maybe there was a mistake. We accused him, he was fired, but money kept going missing," I said. "Maybe he really was a thief though. Maybe Mac saw an opportunity and kept his stealing up after he got fired."

"Maybe," Joanna said, but she was still looking smug.

"The wedding money though, that's incontrovertible. Mac was there. She took the money. The bride recognized her description. Mac was the only person there."

"Except she wasn't, was she?" Joanna said. "Through all of this, there's always been someone else there. Someone who could come and go as she pleased, someone with her own key, someone who didn't need to be on the schedule or rostered because she was always there. Because she owns the place. Someone with a huge shopping addiction and an enormous apartment that she no longer shares with anyone and that she needs to pay upkeep on."

I went cold all over. I swallowed. God, I wanted to believe this. How illogical was that? I wanted to believe that my business partner was stealing from me.

"No, not Addie. I know you don't like her, but..."

"Yes, Addie," Joanna said. "It's the only thing that makes sense. She's always there, this explanation gives you one thief instead of two, and simplicity is always more logical. She needs the money to support all those expensive habits she has. And she wants you back, so blaming Mac was a win-win for her."

"If all that's true, and I'm not saying for a minute that it is, then why the hell did Mac run away?" I said. "Why didn't she stay and defend herself?"

"Is there a chance that she heard the accusations against her?"

I was about to shake my head and then I remembered the office door, just cracked open, as Addie started to talk to me. "Yes," I whispered.

"And what would you have done?" asked Joanna. "She's vulnerable, she's not used to opening up and trusting people, and she knows that you know her history. Do you think she'd have made that leap and trusted you to believe in her?"

I wanted to say yes, but I couldn't. I couldn't because I knew that I hadn't believed in her, that there'd been that awful frozen moment of indecision. Tears were already leaking from my eyes when I turned to Joanna. I'd made such a horrible mistake. I'd screwed everything up.

"What am I going to do?"

"We're going to find out the truth," Joanna said.

"And how exactly do you propose that we do that?" I sniffled but my tears were drying up already. Joanna sounded efficient, like she had a plan. Like she knew how to start fixing all this.

"We start with this guy," she said, pulling a business card from her top pocket and passing it over to me.

I had to read it twice. "A private investigator?" I asked, incredulous.

Joanna grinned. "You want the truth, this guy will find you the truth."

I took a deep breath, looked at the card once more, then nodded. "Let's do this."

Chapter Thirty Two

Mac

I turned on my helpful smile. The one that wasn't too flashy or bright, but that lifted the corners of my mouth enough to make me look nicer, kinder. The woman in front of me winked.

"I don't care about no smile," she said. "I care that you're on time and clean. That's about it. No swearing at the customers and no firearms at work. Those are the rules."

Jesus Christ. What kind of place needed a no firearms at work rule? I looked around the small fast food restaurant. The stink of grease filled my nose and I already knew that my clothes would stink of it as soon as I walked out. Not exactly the insurance office with a water cooler that I had in mind. But I needed this.

"I'm punctual and I'm a fast learner," I said, still with the helpful smile.

"Then we'll get along just fine." She peered over the counter at me. "You know this is just part time, right? My nephew started college and can't do the Tuesday, Wednesday, or Thursday lunch shifts. That's all. We're not talking a full-on job here?"

"That's absolutely fine, ma'am."

Just what I needed. Working a lunch shift would let me get to my waitressing job by five, which in turn let me out just before midnight in time to get to a gig I'd found cleaning offices. The perfect fit.

"Then you come back here tomorrow around ten and I'll give you some training. Not that you'll need much. The job's yours."

I grinned in relief, thanked her, and walked back out into the cool afternoon.

I was making this work. Somehow. I didn't know how the hell other people did it. But it turned out that getting yourself a real kind of job without any sort of degree or experience was harder than hustling the streets for spare change.

With the fast food shifts though, I was pretty much at full time. I'd scrape by enough to pay the motel bill once a week, get food, and start making payments on those debts. With a little extra to put aside for a rainy day.

Yeah, yeah, it sounded like I had my shit together. But I wasn't kidding myself. The big time grown up things like health insurance and eating vegetables every day were going to have to wait.

Still though, I was making a go of it. Eleanor would be proud.

Eleanor.

She still haunted my mind. I couldn't not think about her. How could I? All of this was down to her. And okay, she hadn't turned out to be the right person to put my trust in, but then, how could I have known that? And would I really be in this position, working a real job, feeling secretly proud of myself and like a real adult for once, without her?

Forgiveness is a weakness, that's what Uncle Frank says.

Just for once though, I thought he might be wrong.

One day, a long, long time from now, I wanted to walk into Eleanor's restaurant. I wanted to sit down and order dinner and pay the bill in cash up front. I wanted to order the nice wine, the expensive dessert. I wanted to show her that she'd been right to put her trust in me.

I might not be able to have Eleanor. But I would have my life. A good life. An honest life. I wasn't going to spiral down the drain like my mother had, like Uncle Frank would one day, like, if I was being honest, Mia probably would.

No. I was going to work hard and get what I wanted.

And it had taken Eleanor to show me that I could do that. To show me that I had the strength to do that.

So could I forgive her for not believing in me at the end? Yes. It hurt. But I wasn't moving on into this new life with the old grudges. I was making myself different. Defying fate. And damn, it felt good.

I CAREFULLY CREAKED open the door to the motel room. It wasn't late, barely three in the afternoon. But I never knew when Mia was going to be there and when she wasn't.

"You don't need to creep around," she said, as I opened the door fully.

I recognized the tone in her voice immediately. The short, snippy, argumentative tone she got when she was coming down, when she was starting to freak out about where she was going to get her next hit from.

I swallowed down my anger and smiled brightly. "Just come to change for work," I said.

She was lying on her bed, old TV flashing daytime talk shows on the cabinet. Her hair was stringy, her skin had taken on that grey look again. But she was talking and coherent. That was something.

"Money's on the desk," she said, without looking at me.

I sighed and took the bundle of creased notes from the desk. I didn't want to know what she'd done to get the cash. I told myself she was working odd jobs, picking up gigs where she could. And I'd seen her once at the market a block away, picking up boxes and pushing them onto a van. I could only hope that she wasn't doing anything worse than that.

"My life, my decisions," she said, noticing me staring at the cash. "But if it makes you feel better, it's honestly come by. Swear to God."

I nodded and bundled the money into my jacket pocket. By unspoken agreement, cash didn't get left in the motel room alone with Mia.

Things had been rough since her threat. My own sister threatening to call the cops on me. I knew why she did it, but it took me a good couple of weeks to get used to the idea of her being serious about it. Turns out, it was the kick in the ass that I needed to get my head straight. But we hadn't talked about it.

I'd turned down Frank's offer of work and got started on my job hunt the very next morning. And Mia had insisted on paying her way too.

I knew she was using again. It was pretty inevitable once she had some cash in her pocket. But she'd come up with half the payment for the motel room every week without fail, so I couldn't fault her on that.

I pulled on dark pants. Not even shoplifted. Less than a buck at the thrift store. The restaurant I waitressed at insisted I wear them. And when I turned around, Mia was watching me.

I was struck by a sudden spike of love for her. Despite everything, she pushed herself to do right by me. And it must be so unimaginably hard to be her, to be in the grip of something so much stronger than her willpower.

"Things'll be alright," I said. "Just you wait and see."

She smiled lazily. "I know. I believe in you."

I was about to reply, say maybe she shouldn't, maybe she should let me prove myself first, when there was a knock at the door.

I answered without thinking. A bulky, middle-aged man stood there. He wanted to look harmless, but I could see his eyes darting around, see that he was observing everything. "Ms. Leach?"

I shook my head and he shrugged and grinned.

"Sorry, wrong room." And he trudged away.

I closed the door. Weird.

"That's how they get you," Mia said.

"How who gets me?"

"Debt collectors, paper servers, whoever. They scope you out, find out where you are. Come back later for payment. You shouldn't answer the door without knowing who's knocking first."

"I know."

And I did know. I'd been careless. It wouldn't happen again. The man had seemed harmless enough, I supposed. Except for those observant little eyes flitting this way and that.

Anyway, I was on top of things now. I had money coming in. It wouldn't be long until I had a solid work history and then I could get serious about paying these debts. Get professional help and everything.

It'd be fine. I just needed the debt collectors to hold off until then. Them and the police.

I'd spent a long time after I'd run from Eleanor looking over my shoulder, waiting for the cops to catch me. I was slowly coming to the conclusion that maybe she hadn't called them. But I couldn't be sure.

Yet another reason to be careful about who I opened the damn door too.

"Yeah, sorry about that," I said to Mia. "I'll check the peephole next time."

"Good idea." She was already disappearing back into the TV.

I picked up my bag. "Gotta run." I had a long night's work ahead of me.

Chapter Thirty Three

Eleanor

I watched the sun stream through the window for the last time. The tiled floor of the restaurant was shining clean, the chairs and tables in neat rows. There was no easy way to do what I was about to do, but it was the right thing anyway.

The door opened with a tinkle of the bell, and Addie's shopping bags pushed through before her body. I took a deep breath.

I was standing, not sitting. My bag was already zipped up and ready to go. On the table to my side lay the paperwork that was necessary. Everything had been taken care of.

"You're an early bird," Addie said. "Have you got the coffee machine on already?"

She was bustling toward the back, wanting to lay her shopping bags down, I suppose. "We need to talk."

"Give me a second, darling, let me just—"

"No."

She stopped still, and only then I think, realized that I wasn't sitting, that I wasn't working, that something was different.

I should hate her. Maybe I did a little. I don't know. Maybe I felt sorry for her. Or maybe, more likely, I just felt nothing. For the first time since I'd met her, Addie didn't provoke an emotion in me. Not really.

"What's wrong?" Her voice sounded cautious.

I took a deep breath. No recriminations. No screwing around. Go with your gut and just do it.

"I know everything."

The investigator that Joanna and I had hired had done a fantastic job. He'd accessed Addie's finances and found that just as Joanna had suspected, she'd been the one leaking money from the restaurant. Stealing, I should say. Though I doubt she saw it as stealing, at least at first.

I knew Addie. And I knew that she wasn't evil or criminal or anything else. She was mixed up and confused, broker than she should be, and had probably started out taking just a little cash from the register to tide her over. Then things had grown out of her control. I could see how it could happen.

"Everything about what?" she said, face pale and eyes wide.

She knew exactly what I was talking about, so I didn't bother with an explanation.

"The restaurant is yours," I said. "The paperwork you need is right here. It's all signed. The place is yours to do as you wish with."

"But—but your investment, your money, your..."

"I'm washing my hands of all of this," I said, picking up my bag. "All of this, and you as well. I wish you luck, Addie. Honestly, I do. You're going to need it."

She was shouting my name, but I was already walking away, already opening the door and leaving, never looking back.

Maybe I should have called the police. But I hadn't called them on Mac. Everyone deserves a second chance, even Addie. And she'd be in enough of a bind now, with a restaurant to run and no investor to pump more cash in. I didn't think that trouble with the law was really necessary.

More than that, I didn't feel like giving evidence or talking to the police, or being involved in any way whatsoever. I felt like walking away.

My gut told me that this was the right thing to do. So I listened. Just like Joanna had told me to. My judgment was sound, and if it wasn't, well, this was my mistake to make. And I was sure that I was going to make mistakes, more than one. Changing your life couldn't be flawless.

I stopped two blocks down the street when I saw the first open trash can. Unzipping my bag I upended it over the trash. Accounts and papers from the restaurant fluttered out of the compartment. Yet the bag still felt weighty when I was done.

Unzipping the second compartment I found another bundle of papers. The little ranch house stared out from the first page. With a grin, I withdrew the entire pile and stuffed it into the garbage. No ranch houses for me. No little suburban life for me.

I was going to build something that I wanted. Something that, I hoped, one day Mac would want to live with me. If I ever found her, that is.

And if I didn't find her. Well, my heart would break. But I'd at least be living the life that I wanted. Tasting a little of that rebellion. And making my own definition of a perfect life.

I WALKED THROUGH THE empty rooms. Ceilings towered above me, huge windows stretched the length of the walls. It was cool inside, but the under-floor heating would warm the place nicely in the winter.

Returning to the main living area I turned in a circle. Full fireplace. Stairs stretching up to a mezzanine balcony opening out into two bedrooms. This was by far the most luxurious of the apartments that I'd visited so far.

"What do you think?"

The realtor was a young woman, her hair red and her smile wide. She knew that I loved this place. I nodded. "It's nice," I said, trying to preserve some kind of mystery. I didn't want her to assume I was just going to take the apartment.

It was big. Big enough for a family if it came to that. It was expensive, but not prohibitively so. An investment, definitely, but in an up and coming area of town, so a good investment. My gut was telling me to go for it.

The apartment was a long way from the suburban house I'd been imagining myself in mere months ago. But I could see myself here. I could see Mac here.

I iced up a little inside as I thought of her. No news. Almost three months now and no news at all. But then I guessed that Mac knew how to keep a low profile.

I took one last look around the apartment. Right. This was the place.

"I'd like to talk about making an offer," I said.

The realtor beamed, no doubt thinking of the hefty commission she was about to earn. "Let's take this discussion back to the office, shall we?"

"Absolutely."

The realtor was locking up the front door when my phone rang. I glanced at the number. A habit nowadays, though Addie had stopped calling weeks ago now. Still, it paid to be careful. I noted the number, then apologized to the realtor.

"I have to take this," I said. "I'll meet you back at the car?"

She nodded and set off. I let her get to the end of the corridor before I accepted the call.

"Shepherd."

"Hi, Ms. Shepherd, Don here."

"Got any news?"

There was a minuscule pause and I could hear the PI shuffling papers. My pulse quickened as he cleared his throat. "Found her."

My heart rate soared and I had to close my eyes against the dizziness in my head. Found her. Thank God. I hadn't dared to hope, hadn't dared to think anything other than the fact that maybe she was gone for good. She could have fled the country, she could have been in Canada or Mexico or anywhere else by now.

"I'm sending the details through to your email right now," Don was saying. "Along with my invoice. Unless there's anything else that you need?"

"No," I said, voice shaking. "No, nothing at all. Thank you for all your help."

I'd add a fat bonus to whatever he'd put in his invoice. I could never have done any of this without him.

I disconnected the call, seeing the little email icon in the notification bar. My fingers were trembling.

All I needed to do now was to decide if I was going to see her. If I was going to open this tin of worms. I knew damn well that Mac might not want to see me. I was prepared for that, or I thought I was.

I needed to apologize. That was it. I expected nothing from her. I had no right to expect anything from her. I could try to win her back, but she had every right to turn me down. More than anything though, I needed to tell her how sorry I was. How I never should have doubted her. How I never should have doubted myself.

The email flickered open, the address front and center.

Yes.

Yes. I needed to see her. I was going to see her.

I couldn't do anything else. I couldn't go forward, move on, or try not to love her without seeing her one more time.

It was the only thing I could do.

Chapter Thirty Four

Mac

I was exhausted already, and only one job down. I'd finished my shift at the fast food place, and as expected had stunk of grease and fries. Which meant I had to run back to the motel and shower and change before heading to the restaurant.

Now I just needed to make it through a waitressing shift, then through a four hour office clean, and then, finally, I could sink into bed.

By the time I got into bed these days I was so tired that I couldn't keep my eyes open. So tired that I didn't even dream. Which didn't stop Eleanor's face swimming into my vision before I fell asleep. Maybe it always would.

"Shit."

I almost stumbled over the motel door step in my hurry to get out. I straightened myself, closed the door and made my way out to the sidewalk at a fast pace. I couldn't be late.

For the first time it felt... not warm exactly. But not cold either. For the first time in months I could walk without shoving my hands into my pockets, without worrying about breaking a tooth because I was shivering so hard. Dental insurance. Crap. Yet another thing to add to my list of things I really needed to take care of.

I was so busy trying to remember the last time I'd seen a dentist that I wasn't aware of anything. Not for half a block at least. Not until something stirred in my periphery, until I caught a sound that just wasn't right. Until I felt eyes on me. The hair on the back of my neck rose in prickles.

Without my brain coming into the decision, my feet decided to run.

Eleanor

I sat in my car as the light turned to orange and the evening started to creep in. Mac was in there, I just knew it. I could sense it. Sense her. And I strained to go and knock on that door, practically salivated at the thought of seeing her face again.

But then something stopped me. Fear stopped me. The fear of what would happen, how I would feel, what I would say. What if she slammed the door in my face? How could I deal with that?

"You're here to apologize," I said out loud. "That's all. Just apologize."

I had no right to expect anything else, to hope for anything else. Yet I couldn't help it. A little light of hope still gleamed and if Mac slammed the door in my face that hope would be gone. Extinguished. Forever.

Which was why I couldn't move, why I was frozen.

Until I saw the motel room door open, until I saw a flash of pink and blonde, the movement of a leather jacket. I saw the pieces before I saw the whole. And then Mac was there and my heart stilled inside my body.

It took a long second before I could move. She was half-way out of the parking lot before I even unbuckled my seatbelt.

But once I did, my body took over, my feet slamming onto the tarmac and my hands closing the car door, and my heart following her all the way down the block.

I watched from a distance, breath coming in short gasps, wanting to talk to her, not quite daring to yet, just watching, knowing that she was in the world, knowing that she was a beautiful as magnetic as I remembered. Letting my body be drawn closer and closer until only a few feet separated us.

I was ready for this. I could do this. My mouth was already opening to call her name.

And then she started to run.

Mac

I was on automatic, feet pounding the pavement, breath coming in gulps, my muscles warming to their task.

But my mind was whirling. As soon as I'd started to run, footsteps followed. Who? Who the hell was following me? I didn't dare turn around to see, I could hear how close they were.

The problem was it could have been any one of a hundred people. One of Uncle Frank's minions wanting to punish me for being disrespectful enough to turn down a job. A bailiff. Any one of two dozen creditors. Someone I'd scammed or ripped off, and God knows, there were too many of them to count.

So I just kept on running, weaving through the streets, watching people jump aside as I ran.

How long could I keep this up for?

I was fit enough. But I was also exhausted from working my ass off day after day. I was already ready for bed. And I still had two shifts to work. Hell. What were the chances of me getting to work on time now?

I cursed and put on an extra burst of speed. I was damned if whoever this was was going to lose me a job.

Eleanor

The book-ending of this did not escape me. I'd chased Mac down at the beginning, and here I was, chasing her down again. I just hoped that this wasn't closure. The full circle. I'd chased her to say hello, now I had to chase her to say goodbye.

I was getting into my stride, gaining slowly but steadily. The lead she'd built up when I'd been too frozen to move in the car was decreasing. I could catch her, it was only a matter of time.

But did I want to catch her?

Yes, yes, I did, more than anything. A selfish decision, I knew that, but I had to go with it, it was what every instinct was telling me to do.

I didn't know why she was running from me. Maybe she thought she was in trouble again, maybe she thought that I'd called the cops, tracked her down, wanted to punish her for stealing the money.

I just knew that I had to catch her. If she slapped me, if she spat in my face, if she escaped my clutches, then so be it. But I was going to look her in the eye one more time and apologize properly.

She picked up her pace, and I lengthened my stride to match.

Mac

I was getting close to my limit now.

The streets were emptying out a little, we were getting to a more industrial section of town. I needed to make a decision here.

I couldn't run that much longer, my lungs were telling me that. My heart was about to explode. So I needed a plan B.

Plan B materialized about three seconds after that. A large double door opening into a dark, spacious cavern. Some kind of workshop or something. Darkness was good, darkness meant I could hide. Maybe my chaser would get tired of looking.

Better still, I could see a gleam of light coming from inside the workshop. Whatever the place was, there was another entrance on the other side. The perfect escape route.

I bunched my thigh muscles into one last effort and sprinted for the open door.

The darkness blinded me faster than I was expecting. I tried to slow my pace, was already slowing, and then the ground disappeared out from under me.

My stomach fell through the soles of my feet and my hands scrabbled in panic and I wanted to scream but no noise would come out.

And when my fingers finally grasped onto something I hung in the darkness not knowing where I was or what was happening.

Eleanor

She was there and then she was gone.

She ran into one of the old workshops that dotted this side of the street and I slowed down before I reached the door. Running into dark spaces is never a good idea.

I was already walking when I heard the thump and then the scratching sound of hands. Jesus, something had happened.

"Mac! Mac!"

Her name echoed through the workshop.

"It's me, Eleanor!"

There was a long silence. Then a tired voice shouted "here!"

I turned on the flashlight of my phone, angling it towards the voice. It was coming from an old inspection pit in the center of the floor. I could just see fingertips protruding over the edge.

Carefully, slowly, I made my way over, squatting and shining the light into the pit. "Mac?"

Her eyes glittered more green in the light. "I don't know what the hell you're doing here."

She didn't sound angry. Bemused maybe, confused definitely, but not angry. I didn't know what to say, how to begin explaining myself. Her fingers shifted and a handful of gravel fell into the inspection pit.

I held out a hand. "Let me help you."

There was a long pause. A long, painful pause when I thought that maybe I was going to be heartbroken forever. Maybe my heart would never be fixed.

And then Mac yanked herself up and clasped her hand around my wrist. I pulled with all my might.

She'd let me help.

Chapter Thirty Five

Mac

It's difficult to be angry when someone has just pulled you out of the pits of hell.

Or an inspection pit, whatever.

I wanted to be angry, don't get me wrong. Everything in my head said that I should be angry. Angry that Eleanor hadn't believed me, angry that she'd chased me, angry that she'd let me go.

But in the end, she hadn't let me go, had she? I'd run away. I'd run away instead of facing my problems and dealing with them, and that wasn't her fault, it was mine.

"I'm sorry."

We were sitting on the edge of the pit, legs dangling into the darkness, both recovering our breath. There was no sign of whoever owned the place, but then there wasn't really anything here. No tools, nothing. So maybe it was abandoned.

"I'm sorry," I said.

"No." Eleanor took such a deep breath that I could hear it. "Let me do this, Mac. Please. It's important."

" 'kay." I needed to calm myself anyway. I could barely trust myself to speak.

"I'm sorry. I should have believed in you more. I'm sure you overheard what happened in the office, with Addie accusing you of stealing. I should have jumped to your defense. Because I did believe in you. Deep down, I really did. And I'm sorry for chasing you and frightening you. But most of all, I'm sorry for not trying to find you sooner."

I swallowed. It was a lot to take in. But she wasn't the only one with apologies to make. "I'm sorry. I'm sorry that I ran away instead of trusting in you to believe me. I'm sorry for running from you. I'm sorry for making your life harder than it needed to be."

Still we sat. It was getting even darker. Colder. Eleanor cleared her throat. I was still breathless, but not from running. I was breathless because she was sitting beside me because I didn't know what she was going to say because I was afraid she wouldn't want me and afraid that she would. Despite the cold, I was beginning to sweat. My legs itched to run away again, but I wouldn't let them.

"There's something else," Eleanor said. "I don't know if you want to hear it. But I need to say it. I—" She looked around and grimaced. "This isn't exactly the kind of place I imagined this happening."

She took my hand in hers, cool skin meeting warm skin. And suddenly I knew what she was going to say. I knew and the fear left me, drained away leaving me light and soaring.

"Mac, I love you."

And there it was. Said. Out there loud and proud in the world and nothing could take it back. And nothing had ever made me feel so complete. I looked down at my hands, absently catching the time on my watch as I did.

"Oh, shit." I jumped to my feet.

"What? I'm sorry Mac, I didn't mean to go too fast. It's fine if you don't—"

I caught hold of her arm. "Stop. No. It's nothing like that. I love you too. I have to go. I'm late for work."

See how I just slid that in there? Right in the middle of other stuff like it wasn't the most important thing I'd ever said in my life? Smooth, right? But that's how it is. Love, when it comes is so comfortable, so fitting, that it doesn't need a special time or place to be admitted. It just is. You can say it whenever or wherever and it will still have the same power, the same weight, the same meaning.

"Work?" Eleanor frowned.

"Work," I said. "A job. Two jobs actually. Well, three but I've already worked one today so there's two left and—"

"And nothing. Go. I understand." She reached into a pocket and pulled out a card, thrusting it into my hand. "Meet me here when you're done."

I looked at the card, then back at Eleanor. "It won't be until much, much later. Maybe three o'clock."

"I don't care. Just come. Please. I don't want to spend another night without you."

I ran all the way to work. And I wasn't late.

Eleanor

The night stretched on and on and I sat in that big new living room, the ceilings towering above me, a fire flickering in the fireplace and wondered what would happen if she didn't come.

The thought of the sun rising and having to face the fact that she'd chosen not to come was physically painful.

No book could entertain me, no music could capture my attention. So I sat in the silence, firelight dancing on the walls and waited.

Waited to see if she was strong enough to come back to me.

Waited to see if my gut reaction had been right.

Waited for so long that when the doorbell finally rang I didn't recognize the sound of it for a moment.

"What's this place?"

Her eyes stared around curiously, taking in the new apartment, taking in the furniture, the fire, the windows, everything.

"It's a new start," I said.

And I sat her down and told her everything. About the restaurant, about Addie, about the stealing, and about walking away. And about my new plan. My new life.

"I needed to have more confidence in myself," I said, finally. "And you taught me that. After making such huge mistakes with Addie, with the restaurant, I felt like I couldn't trust my own judgment. Which is stupid."

"It is," she said. "It is, but I can understand it. I mean, I wouldn't trust me as far as I could throw me, and I'm me. So, you know, I guess I get why you might not immediately jump to my defense."

"But I should. I would. Given a chance to do things over." She said nothing but shuffled a little closer on the couch. "Tell me about you," I said. "What have you been doing?"

She filled me in and I listened to the calming sound of her voice. Listened and was amazed at what she had done, how she had turned her life around, how hard she was working. And I told her so.

"It was you," she said, simply. "You showed me what I could have. If I could be bothered to take it. If I could stop looking for easy answers and quick fixes." She took my hand. "I'm not going to lie. It's tough as hell. I'm barely on top of things. But I'm doing this, I'm taking control. And it feels good."

I clasped her hand tight in mine, feeling her pulse through her fingers.

"What now?" she asked.

What now indeed. Should I ask now? Should I speak now? Or should I wait, wait until we knew each other better, wait until we'd built bridges and strengthened what was still a precarious relationship?

Now.

It had to be now.

"I'd like this to be home."

"What?"

I took a deep breath. "Mac, I want this apartment to be home. For us. I've spent so long trying to live the perfect life, so long thinking I had to do things a certain way. And I'm tired of it. I don't want to live that way. I want to be happy. And it's become abundantly clear to me that being happy involves being with you. For now, at least, maybe forever, I don't know. What I do know though, is that I don't want a ranch house in the suburbs and two kids and a station wagon. I want this. Us. Here."

"A ranch house?" Mac asked, half-grinning at me. "Who mentioned a ranch house?"

"It's not important." I pulled her closer. "Mac, move in here. We can help each other. We improve each other. Surely, you see that?"

She looked at the fire, her face a picture of concentration. I wanted to kiss the little bow of her top lip.

"I need to pay my own way," she said.

"We'll figure out the finances. But I assure you, you won't be dependent on me."

"Not financially anyway."

"Okay."

"It's taken a long time to come to this," Mac said.

I raised my eyebrows in surprise. "Really? And here was I thinking we were moving awfully fast. But in a good way."

"That's not what I meant," she said, smiling. "I meant that it's taken me a long time to realize that it's not a question of needing someone else. It's a question of wanting them. I don't need you, Eleanor. And that's a good thing. I don't want to be with someone because I need them. I want to be with them because I want them. Does that make sense?"

I nodded. "It does. Perfect sense."

She stood up, her back to me, outlined by the firelight, delicate and fragile and strong and beautiful. When she walked, her hips swayed gently and I was so hypnotized by them that I almost didn't realize what was happening.

"Where are you going?" I said, suddenly shocked into speaking.

She was leaving, running away again. This was all too much, too fast.

Mac turned around.

"I'm going to bed," she said.

She held out a hand, fingers outstretched toward me. "Are you coming?"

Epilogue

Mac

My stomach was jumping as I pushed open the door. Stupid, I know. But I knew Eleanor well enough to know that I didn't know how she was going to react to a possible sudden change in our circumstances.

"Give me a second!" Eleanor shouted.

I could see that she was just putting the finishing touches to a cake, her hands were gloved, and her tongue stuck out in that cute way it always did when she was concentrating.

"Ugh, hey Mac." Joanna was rummaging in her bag with one hand, and then she suddenly looked up at me. "Sorry, that 'ugh' wasn't for you, I swear. Here, hold him for a second, would you."

And before I knew it, I had an armful of wriggling baby.

Leigh was all of three months old and frankly, still looked a lot like Winston Churchill. Not that I'd told Joanna that. She was Eleanor's best friend, I didn't exactly want to get on her bad side. Besides, I liked her. She made me laugh. And Leigh was growing on me.

Hold up there. Not enough that I wanted one of my own. No way, no how.

But enough that I kind of liked holding his wiggly warmth and wouldn't mind babysitting once in a while.

"Finally," Joanna said, pulling a bottle out of her bag and taking the baby back from me. "You look pooped. Long day at work?"

I rolled my eyes. "You know, these car accident scams are getting harder and harder."

"I do wish you wouldn't talk like that in front of company," Eleanor said, snapping off her gloves and surveying her cake with pride. "I swear

185

you take pleasure in making the innocent public think that you're still a scam artist."

"Joanna isn't the innocent public," I pointed out.

"Indeed I'm not," said Joanna, primly. "I am, however, starved of intelligent and interesting conversation since Leigh refuses to discuss anything other than poop or food with me. So feel free to regale me with your most juicy stories."

"You're going back to work next week," Eleanor put in. "And you'll have all the adult conversation you need."

"Not cool stories about scams and insurance fraud though," pouted Joanna.

I grinned. The job was perfect. More than perfect. And I'd worked my way up. It had started with Don, the private investigator Eleanor and Joanne had hired to find me. A man I recognized when I met him as the bulky guy that had knocked on the motel door one afternoon. He'd called me in for a consultation about someone he was investigating. And things had kind of spiraled from there.

Now I had a desk, a cubicle, and a job title. Helping a nationally known insurance company combat fraud. I got a pay-check, and even had health insurance. Not bad for a drop out.

I knew how lucky I was. But I also knew how hard I'd worked.

"I'll save the best stories for next weekend," I promised. "You and Lucas are still coming over for dinner, right?"

"Wouldn't miss it for the world." Leighton's eyes were closing. "You know, I'd better get him home while he's quiet. I hate walking down the sidewalk with him screaming in his pushchair. I get paranoid that people are going to think I'm doing something horrible to him."

She bundled the baby into his seat and we said our goodbyes. I caught her just by the door. "Don't react to anything you see outside that door," I hissed, careful that Eleanor couldn't hear.

"Huh?"

"Trust me. I'll explain everything later."

The baby wailed and then settled and Joanna hustled out of the door.

"So, are we done here?" I asked.

Eleanor was tidying up and I flipped the sign on the door to closed. One of the nice things about Eleanor owning a bakery rather than a restaurant was that people generally didn't want cupcakes at seven in the evening. So she closed at six and then I had her all to myself. Unless she was working on a wedding cake, of course.

"Almost done," she grinned.

"I'll take care of things and close up," said a voice from the back.

"Hi, Tom!"

"Hey, Mac." He pushed his tousled blonde head around the doorway to grin at me. "Want to hit that new bouldering place on Thursday?"

"Sounds like a plan."

"I'll text you later then."

Tom had been the obvious choice when Eleanor opened the bakery, and he'd leaped at the chance to work with her again. Surprising, considering she'd fired him once already and falsely accused him of theft. But forgiveness was a miraculous thing, as I was discovering myself.

God, I hoped Eleanor was going to forgive me for what was about to happen.

She was chattering happily as she pulled on her coat, talking about a new recipe she was trying, and I let her talk. I didn't stop her until we were right in front of the door.

"Hold on a second," I said. "Um..."

I'd wanted to prepare her, but now I didn't really know what to say. I didn't know because I honestly had no idea how she was going to react. This wasn't something we'd discussed.

"Um, what?" she asked.

Her eyes were deep blue and wide and so innocent looking that I wanted to take her in my arms and keep her safe from the world Instead I pulled her close and kissed her soundly.

"I just wanted you to know that whatever happens, I love you."

Now those eyes sparkled. "Whatever happens? Intriguing..." She looked at the door, then back at me. "Is this anything to do with what you were whispering to Joanna about before she left."

"You caught that, huh?"

She just grinned. "I don't miss much."

I stood back and cringed as she reached for the door handle and pulled. Please, please let her want this as much as I did.

Eleanor

I looked down at the puppy snuggled on the rug in front of the fire. "What about Jim?"

"Too normal," Mac said.

She was sitting beside me, her eyes glued to the dog and I couldn't help but smile. She obviously adored him, and had equally obviously been terrified that I would make her give him up. Fortunately, the second that I'd opened the door and seen him tied up outside with an old piece of rope I'd fallen just as much in love with him as Mac had.

"Where did you find him again?"

"Uh, behind that bodega, you know the one on the corner across from my office?"

"There you go then. Bodega. That's a great name for a dog. What do you think, Bo?"

The puppy opened up one eye and then rolled over, luxuriating in the warmth of the fire.

"Eleanor, can we talk about something?"

My heart pattered in a panicked rhythm. I'd thought everything was going so well, I'd thought we were doing great together. What could the problem be? Was she unhappy? Was... I took a deep breath.

I needed to stop this. Needed to stop doubting myself, doubting Mac. We were happy. I knew we were happy.

"Sure," I said easily. "What's on your mind?"

"Selling the apartment."

I did a double take. "What? Are you kidding? Do you have any idea how much this place cost? What an investment it was?"

"Eleanor, it's not about that."

"It is, of course it is. I realize that not everything is about money. But this is. It has to be. I—"

But she was already standing up, already walking away. I held my breath, held my tongue. But she didn't make for the front door. That was the old Mac. The new Mac calmly and slowly walked off towards the bedroom.

Shit.

I'd said the wrong thing. Despite everything, money was still an issue between us. It sort of had to be. There was no getting over the fact that we were in financially very different positions. We'd had some awkward conversations over the last few months, and our fair share of arguments as well.

But we were getting there, slowly. We were figuring out ways to make things work. Mac was paying off her debt, was paying down the amount owed on Mia's rehab. She was working full time and earning a decent salary. The bakery was doing okay, it wasn't going to make me rich, but that wasn't why I was doing it.

All in all, I'd thought we were doing better. Until this. Until I screwed things up by speaking without thinking.

I took a few deep breaths and looked down at Bo. He was still sleeping, so I left him to it and followed Mac into the bedroom.

"I'm sorry," I said. She was sitting on the bed. "I over-reacted and I didn't listen to you. That was rude. This is something we should talk about and decide together. Why do you think we should sell the apartment?"

I could see that she was angry, but also that she was trying to put her anger aside. It was something that I respected about her, a side that was relatively new.

"I think we should sell the apartment so that we can buy a place together."

Jesus. Now I felt even worse. "Buy a place together? Are you sure?"

She nodded. "My credit score is improving, I'm on top of my finances. And I'd like to contribute more. I'd like a home that's ours, that we buy together, rather than one that's yours."

I knew what she meant. It hurt, and I'd never thought of this apartment as anything other than ours. But I got it. I knew how important this was to her.

"Fine."

"What?" Her eyes were shining and her face was paler than normal.

"Fine."

"Just like that?"

"Just like that. What are we looking for? Something smaller. Bigger? What part of town do you want to look in? We'll need to decide these things, you know."

I sat down on the bed next to her. She was flushing, her warmth, her smell, were so intoxicating. I put my hand on her leg.

"What about something different?"

"Like what?"

She cleared her throat. "I was thinking maybe, well, what about something with a garden? Something where the puppy, I mean Bo, can play outside? Something a little less... A little less city."

It was my turn to frown. "Something... suburban?" I could hardly believe I was saying that word to Mac.

She turned to look at me. "Would that be so bad?"

And I laughed. I laughed so hard that she stopped looking angry and instead started looking worried.

"We don't have to if you don't want to, Eleanor. It was just an idea. I just thought with Joanna and Lucas moving out of the city too, and with the puppy, and with Mia coming out of rehab soon and needing a clean start, I thought it might be time for us too. Time to move on a stage. To grow up a little."

"To move out to the suburbs."

She nodded.

"How many dogs are you thinking about getting?" I asked.

"Bo's enough for now." She shot me a glance. "But I wouldn't mind a couple of cats."

"So we can be stereotypical lesbians?" I grinned. "Okay."

"Okay?"

"Okay. If this is the life you want then let's look into it."

She took my hands in hers. "Is it the life you want though?"

I thought hard. I'd been thinking hard. I'd come a long way, changed a lot since I'd met Mac.

"You know, I don't think I want any specific kind of life," I said. "As long as I'm with you, everything else is just... side dishes. I spent too long thinking life had to go a certain way. Now I think it should go however you want it to go. So why not? Why not give this a try? If we don't like it, we can always move back to the city."

"Or try getting more dogs."

"Which could very well help persuade me to like a place more," I agreed.

I was leaning in to kiss her when the sound of anxious barking interrupted. We both stood and flew to the top of the stairs. Standing on the mezzanine balcony looking down at the living room we could see Bo barking his little head off and struggling to get up the stairs. Mac rushed to pick him up.

"You know, we're going to need to look at houses without stairs," she said as she carried him up. "I don't think his little legs can manage them."

"You mean a ranch house?" I asked, raising an eyebrow.

"Yeah, if that's what you call them."

I shook my head and sighed.

"What?" asked Mac.

"I just never realized that wanting the very opposite of you would end up so perfectly," I said. "Next thing you'll be telling me that you're going to let your hair grow back it's natural color."

"Never," she said, stoutly, putting Bo down so he could explore the bedroom. She came to stand in front of me, to loop her arms around my neck. "Did you really want the opposite of me?"

I smiled a little, pulling her closer. "No," I said. "No, I don't think I did. I think I just didn't realize what I did want."

"And what's that?" Her lips were chillingly close to mine, skin brushing skin.

"You," I whispered, letting our lips finally meet.

Also by Sienna Waters

The Opposite of You
Love By Numbers

Watch for more at https://www.siennawaters.com/.

About the Author

I've always loved romance, any kind of romance. But growing up, I could never find the exact kind of romance I wanted, the kind of romance about people like me. So I decided to write it myself. My books are about two people falling in love, just like all romances are. But in my case, those two people just happen to both be women. And all my stories have a happy ending, because I truly believe that there's a happy ending out there waiting for everyone.

When I'm not writing I'm spending far too much time online shopping, trying to persuade my cats to dress up, and trying to persuade my wife that I'm not as crazy as I sometimes appear (she believes this about half the time, the other half of the time she just puts up with me with endless patience).

If you'd like to know more about me, or you'd like to stay up to date with new releases, then subscribe to my newsletter here: http://eepurl.com/dOyZBv

Thank you for reading!

Read more at https://www.siennawaters.com/.

Milton Keynes UK
Ingram Content Group UK Ltd.
UKHW012145040124
435404UK00004BA/146